Take a trip with Quill Vance to the world of Appalachia before the technology revolution.

Watch with Quill as Dad and Will Gorman send a passel of con men packing.

Meet Mattie, the new school teacher with more than one big problem.

Learn how lovable and loyal a mongrel dog can be.

See two young boys from two different worlds come together at the same time and place.

Be there when Quill has his first taste of love, or what he perceives it to be.

Help Quill keep his friend Ceece from getting them tarred and feathered.

Spend the day with Elmer C. Spinsworthy, the last true Drummer to pass through these mountains.

Join a fire fighting crew when it seems like the whole world will burn.

CONTENTS

WILL GORMAN -- Stock-Swapper

"Them blame pin-hookers are stealing from the farmers around here again," Dad said.

"Every month, you go to the cattle sale, come back with the same tale," Mama said. "Did they beat you out of any money?"

"Well, no, but they did some of the others. If we don't do something about them soon, the sale barn will close and folks around here won't have no place to sell their stock. No way and can we afford to haul them all the way to Knoxville, Greenville, Chattanooga, or Atlanta."

"Then why don't you go over to Cold Cabin Creek and ask Will Gorman for help?"

"Woman, he's the shystiest trader in these here parts."

"I've heard you say that many a time. Appears to me that's exactly what you need."

"Well, if that don't beat a hen a'crowin." Dad looked at me. "Quill! Quill! I don't know what you've done to my razor. How you dulled it shavin that peach fuzz on your face is beyond me!"

"I sharpened it on your leather strop--"

"You sure you didn't use a file or a rasp? I'll take you with me to the sale next time and get you one of your own."

"Quill combs his hair twenty times a day," my next-to-youngest sister said. "He gets all gussied up ever single night. He's turned into a sissy."

Dad went to the bee house like he always did when he got mad. "Gonna clean me some bee gums."

"Went to his pouting house," Mama said, when my younger sister asked where Dad was.

"Why don't he like Will Gorman?" I said.

"Folks say they're a strange lot."

"How come?"

"Keep to themselves, they do--save for Will. He gets out and about."

"Where do they live?" I asked her.

"Way back up above Footers. Place called Cold Cabin Creek."

Dad came to the house well after dark. He seemed in a better way; he even turned on the battery radio for a spell. I could smell the faint odor of rhubarb wine on his breath. "I'm going to see Will Gorman," he said. "Got me an idea."

"When?" Mama said.

"Next sale day."

"What are pin-hookers?" I said.

"Bunch of scoundrels that follow the livestock auctions. They hang around outside the barn.

2

When a farmer drives up they try to buy his stock at a low price."

"They don't have to sell to them," I said.

"I'll take you with me next time," Dad said. "You'll see."

The next month we took a sow, three shoats, and a milk cow belonging to our neighbor to the McAllen farm. It was the only farm in these parts with a big barn. They had the only bottomland hereabouts, too. McAllen even had a silo and a steam-driven tractor. The farm lay south of the county seat on the good road, and they held a sale there every third Monday in the month.

Some men I never seen before stood along the drive from the road to the barn. They jumped on the side of our truck and climbed up so they could see the stock. They hung on as Dad drove toward the sale barn. Questions flew so fast I couldn't track who was asking what.

"What would you take for the cow?"

"She easy milked?"

"What do you reckon she'll bring?"

"Is she bred back?"

"How old is she?"

"How much milk do she give?"

"When she due to come in fresh?"

"Don't belong to me," Dad said. "I got word to run her through the sale."

"You might get a bid on her," said a man with his foot on the running board of Dad's truck. "I doubt it."

By then, there was a good dozen of them, all-- talking faster than water runs over rocks on the Konehetta River.

"How much for the sow?"

"Is she yourn?"

"How old is she?"

"What'll she go, you reckon? Two hundred?"

"How big was her last litter?"

Dad backed the truck up to the loading dock as the men went right on with their prying. Dad never let on they was there.

"Is them shoats hern?"

"Them shoats the only pigs she had?"

"Set a price on her. What'll you take for the shoats?"

"Price of pork's down, you know."

Dad stood at the back of the truck and spoke to the man who owned the barn. "Unload'em."

"Thanks," Mr. McAllen said, and swung our tailgate open. "They've run off half my trade. Packing house buyers, they've threatened to quit coming if something ain't done about them."

"I'll bet," Dad said.

"Who was them men?" I asked Dad, while we looked over the stock from the overhead walkway.

"They're the pin-hookers I told you about--the ones that try to buy the stock cheap, soon as its

4

owner shows up here. Then they haul the stock off to the big sales in Atlanta or Knoxville."

"But why do people sell to them? Why don't they do like you just did?"

"Some folks confuse easy. Others are afraid they won't get a fair bid inside. After the sale, them pin-hookers won't give them anything."

"Won't the pin-hookers bid?"

"That's another thing. They start the bidding so low, many a time the owner has to no-sale his stock. Then the owner has to pay the sale fee anyway. Or else he'll have to take the low bid because he don't have the dollar sale fee."

"What about the other buyers?"

"The pin-hookers bid on their own stock, drive up the price, for sure if a local man wants to bid on some brood stock."

When Dad went down to the sale floor, I pondered what he had told me. Later I climbed down and stood by the side of the barn where I could hear through a crack in the wall what the pin-hookers said.

It was plain the pin-hookers knew more about stock than the farmers did. They could guess the weight of a cow within thirty pounds, a hog even better, a calf within just a few pounds. They also knew the market price per pound the packinghouses were willing to pay.

Twice I heard them make money just by lying to folks. One they lied to was an old lady from up our way. Her man had died two weeks before. Her son Roy was with her. He stuttered so bad only the old lady could understand a thing he said. He was three years younger than me and wouldn't speak to any stranger, or much to any one else.

It made me mad as fire when they told her she would have to pay ten dollars up front. "You have to pay to get your milk cow examined by the county inspector before you can sell it inside. Give you twenty dollars, right now," a pin-hooker said. "That way, you see, I'll pay the up-front money."

"Psst, Roy!" I whispered through the crack.

He looked around, like it scared him--afraid the voice was going to ask him something.

"Roy, it's me, Quill Vance. Don't let her sell that cow so cheap. The county don't charge no inspection fee."

He walked over and looked through the crack. He grinned when he recognized me but didn't say anything.

"That cow's worth three times that money," I said. "Go tell your mama."

Roy walked back over to where his mother was still talking to the pin-hooker. He stood beside her for a little while. Twice I saw him touch her on the arm, but he couldn't bring himself to speak up in front of the stranger.

I took off running for Dad--got all the way to the rear door before I saw him a hundred yards down in a field with some men. I turned and ran back to the crack in the wall.

"Icing on the cake," the pin-hooker said as the woman and Roy drove off in their old truck.

An hour later a big truck drove up with a pair of fine red mules so tall their heads stuck well above the cab. A jersey cow stood against the tailgate.

The pin-hookers barely looked as they passed. It was a big cow. I couldn't figure why they didn't try to buy her.

The driver, who was about Dad's size and age, had on a black felt hat and wore horn-rimmed glasses. A boy my age started unloading the truck by himself. He led the cow into the first stall on the left.

One mule brayed three times and backed up against the truck cab. The other mule stood to one side, stretched out his neck, and opened his mouth. "He-haw. He-haw. He-haw-he-haw."

All at once they tore out of the truck bed--must have jumped thirty feet. They ran down the hall. I knew they'd break their fool necks when they hit the log fence at the far end.

"Whoa. Gee, Jake," the boy said, not very loud.

The mules slid to a stop and turned into a stable on the right. The boy walked down and closed the gate.

"He must of raised them from colts," I heard a man behind me say.

7

Most of the men who handled the stock carried a long walking stick; some even had a small leather whip. This man and boy had neither.

The bullpen was down next to the far end of the hall. Close to twenty bulls pushed and shoved each other; some tried to hook their horns in the yellow locust barn wall. Most of the stock was raised here in the mountains, and they had never been around people much. Some ran wild all year except in the heart of winter.

The man climbed over the log wall and walked among the bulls, rubbed their backs, and looked them over real close. One big yellow bull backed into a corner and pawed the ground--slung dirt up against the high ceiling.

I batted my eyes and my mouth flew open when the man walked straight up to the bull and rubbed his knuckles between its horns. The bull calmed right down. The man spent another five minutes in the bullpen before he climbed out over the fence. Soon as he was out, the big yellow bull bawled and shook his head, like he wanted to fight.

"My name's Calvin, Calvin Gorman." The boy had walked up beside me, while my eyes were fixed on the man and the bulls.

We talked a long time. I told him about the pin-hookers. He listened, but didn't make a judgment.

When the sale started a few minutes later, the pin-hookers did just what Dad said they'd do. As they drove the price up, the packinghouse buyers looked more and more nervous; they squirmed and mopped their brows like it was hot in the barn.

"Can I go home with Calvin?" I said, the following month. "We ain't got much to do around here, til tobacco cutting time."

Mama said it was all right. Dad had not said for sure, two days before the next sale.

Mama packed me some britches in a flour sack the day before, just in case. Dad still didn't sound favorable, but the next morning he said yes. Seemed like he sometimes changed his mind about things after him and Mama slept on it.

This time Calvin's mother came with them to the sale barn. She was a pretty little lady with black hair put up in a bun with long hairpins. She stayed away from the crowd, nodded to the other women when they passed.

"Mother ain't a deaf mute, but she is deaf," Calvin said. "Just make sure she can see your face when you speak."

By the time we reached Miller's Mill, I could talk to her like anybody else. She did sound a little peculiar: like a child almost, but she told so many funnies we laughed until my sides ached.

Will carried an armload of clean flour sacks into the store.

"Your turn of corn's on the porch," the miller said, when Mrs. Gorman walked in the door.

"I thank ye," she said. "We'll have the usual."

The storekeeper brought out five pounds of coffee, a big sack of flour, a sack of rice, a box of soda, and I don't know what-all else. He toted stuff until the counter was out-and-out full of goods. He went into the back and brought out a quarter of a hoop of cheese.

"Will there be anything else," Mrs. Gorman?

She pulled a snow-white five-pound flour sack from her purse. "Thank ye to fill this sack with horehound candy."

Mr. Gorman walked up with a cardboard box of horseshoes and a half a keg of nails. "There's two more boxes in the back," he said to Calvin. "And a horse collar."

It took a good spell to load all the things they had bought. It covered the whole front of the truck bed three feet deep.

"Reckon you don't stop here often," I said.

"Every month or oftener," Calvin said.

"How many brothers you got?"

"Seven brothers. And two sets of twin sisters," he said. "Fourteen in all. I'm the youngest. Some live on up the valley but they usually eat at our house."

"How old are the girls?"

"They're older than us boys. And married, too."

I wanted to tell Will Gorman about the pinhookers, but thought better about it until I learned more about the Gorman family. The way them pin-hookers swindled Roy and his mama still played on my mind as much as it did when it happened. I hoped Dad and Will could run them off. It seemed like they were taking their sweet time about it.

We passed the last settlement on Footers Creek around four that evening, and were still riding and climbing when dark came. We hadn't seen a smoking chimney in over an hour when the outline of a large building came into sight. It looked might-near the size of our church house.

"Now that's a big house," I said.

Calvin laughed. "That's the barn, the house ain't near that big."

He was right; the house was smaller, but not by much. Even in the dark, I could see it had two wings that went out from the sides, and a porch that wrapped all the way around.

Next morning they called us to breakfast at four-thirty. One whole wing of the house was set up for cooking and eating. The eating room, which measured maybe twenty feet by twenty feet, had two big homemade tables covered with food. A small wash pan full of biscuits sat in the center of each.

The two sets of twins served grits, gravy, fried potatoes, country ham, sausage, and hoecakes. The smell of fresh-brewed coffee from a gallon pot filled the room. It hissed loud as Mrs. Gorman took it off the big wood cook stove.

After we ate, we walked out on the south porch. I looked around at the high mountain valley. It had to be close to a half a mile wide and a mile long. I'd never guess that a valley that big was hid so high up in the Snowbird Mountains.

Calvin and me went down to watch the older boys work their stock. They led two young mules hooked to a sled around a well-worn path.

"Firm but fair," Will said. "Above all, slow and gentle with the young'uns."

"How'd you folks ever find this place?" I said.

"Why, we been here forever and a day," Calvin said. "I've never heard any body put a time on it."

We helped Mr. Gorman with the blacksmithing. That is, we drilled holes in huge locust runners to make a sled for a yoke of oxen.

After a while Calvin and me slipped off and rode some steers: a blue-black pole and a roan that were as well trained as any horses. At first, It scared me--I'd never rode anything but a mule and Ol' Sally, our logging horse.

"What do you do with so much stock?" I said.

"The good'uns, Dad tries to sell around here," Calvin said. "The plugs, he takes to the flat country like Alabama or Georgia or sometimes Florida."

"When does he take'em?"

"In the fall. Farmers don't buy things when they need'em. They buy when they've got money. And that's in the fall, when they sell their crops."

Come early fall, I found out how Will Gorman could sell the old plugs to the big farmers down in the flat country. He doctored the horses with special shoes if they had trouble walking. We washed the stock every two days. We curried them night and morning. Will mixed up special feed for each one, and we worked them four hours a day. They got to looking a hundred times better.

"Is Will going to file their teeth down, to make them look younger?" I said to Calvin.

"No, but we'll make them as fat and healthy as we can."

The strangest thing was what Will fed them every morning as soon as he went in the barn. It took him a half an hour to make up the concoction. He poured sweet feed in a number one washtub and mixed in stuff from three big black jugs. He added enough molasses to make it all stick together in balls about the size of a sock full of rags. The sweet smell filled the barn from the rafters to the floor. He gave balls to the horses, mules, and steers as soon as he finished. That stock had a hankering for it like a spoiled kid does for candy.

I figure the main thing in the balls was white liquor. Whatever it was, the smell was strong and sweet. At any rate, the stock sure had a craving for the stuff.

Come near time for him to go, Will asked Dad if I could go with him and Calvin to sell the stock.

13

They'd told me and I'd read that it was all bottomland down there. I wanted to see a place where you could plow a field without having to stay with the lay of the land. I'd even heard tell you could plow in a circle.

I nearly fell over when Dad didn't take any time in answering. "I guess it would be all right."

The next Monday, we drove the stock over to the depot where the Nantahala River joins the Tennessee. It was late in the evening when we loaded the horses and mules into some boxcars that had sides like a corncrib. I didn't say anything, but they must have been made to haul stock.

Will shut the last boxcar door and led us to the car that had sleeping quarters with curtains. "You two take this berth. The train leaves in fifteen minutes."

Will, he went off to the dinning car while me and Calvin ate the rest of the ham-biscuits and apples Mrs. Gorman had packed.

We slept until just after daybreak when Will came and shook us. "When we stop to take on water the next time, I want you with me in the cattle cars."

"What for?" I said.

"At the Saluda grade the train will be going down a steep mountain. We need to see the stock don't bunch up and cripple one another."

While the train took on water, Calvin showed me how to tie ropes across the cars to keep the stock apart. Will gave us a flour sack with some sweet balls in it. We got into the rear car and climbed up against the roof. It scared me a little, but I never let on as the train started down the mountain. We busted the sweet balls and threw them up near the high end of the car. With our feet, we shoved the stock around when they bunched up. By the time the train leveled off, the sweat was rolling off our faces.

Calvin climbed down. "We can go get us some breakfast."

One old mule must have figured out that the ride was going to be easier now that we were on level ground, for he lit out a braying. "He-haw, he-haw, he-haw-he-haw."

The third day, when we stopped to let the stock out of the cars to stretch for an hour, we were in some of the biggest fields that ever was. I didn't let on, but there wasn't a hill or tree as far as I could see.

The fourth day we pulled in at a depot in a town and Will came by. "Get your things. This is were we unload."

I was so busy looking at the land I never got the name of the place. Will rented a big barn to put the stock up in. After we fed and curried them, he led us over to a boarding house on the north side of the tracks.

The next morning Will passed out the sweet balls while we curried and tended the stock. After that, he sent us to nail up some signs that said STOCK SALE SATURDAY. Later Will went all over town putting out the word at every feed store and business. By week's end, the word was out all over that county.

A few farmers came by but Will kept the barn locked and wouldn't let them in.

"Why don't he show them off every chance he gets?" I said as we sat on the boarding house porch the next evening.

"Wait and see," Calvin said.

On Saturday, the sale day, Will entered the barn early, and walked through, holding one of the sweet balls in his right hand. He didn't give the stock any. When the first farmers got there, the horses and mules brayed and pranced around like a bunch of colts. In no time, the barn was full of farmers.

"That stock got a lot of life in them," A farmer said.

"Must be young," Another allowed.

As each one was brought into the ring, Will stood against the wall with a sweet ball in his hand. I could smell it way back where I was. The braying mule let go another long "He-haw-he-haw-he-haw."

The sorriest old horse mule sold for over eighty dollars. All the rest must have brought what Will

16

wanted. As soon as the sale was over he went to the bank and settled up. Thirty minutes later we boarded the train for home.

I was sure Dad and Will could tear them pin-hookers up somehow--if they would set their minds to it. Only thing was, Will never mentioned them and Dad didn't go to the sale much anymore. He claimed there wouldn't be many pin-hookers there this time of year.

All my life I'd heard many a trading tale about Will Gorman. Some were pretty far-fetched.

One Saturday down at the mill a man told a tale. "Thar was this man who went to ask about buying a young milk cow off that Will Gorman fellow. Will told him, 'When we got this heifer, the kids milked her in a tin cup. Now they have to milk her in a ten-quart bucket.'

"The man bought the cow and took her home. When his wife went to milk, she didn't get enough to cover the bottom of the bucket. So, the man went back on Will. 'Didn't you say when you got this cow the kids milked her in a tin cup and now they have to use a ten-quart bucket?'

"'I sure told you that,' says Will. 'The kids lost the tin cup.'"

There was this man from here by the name of Vondell Strubbs. He was a large man who lived a little piece out of town on farmland his granddaddy had got through a land grant. Folks knew he was an only child from an only child, so his bragging on his things and stuff got their dander up.

With Vondell's nature being what it was, he had a hard time even hiring a teamster to turn his ground. Even though he had money, most of the men wouldn't work for him. They'd rather skid pole wood off the mountains for a dollar a cord.

"He throws off on everything that ain't his'n," a teamster told us one day when he stopped by the creek to water his horses. "Besides which, you cain't never do enough to please him."

Vondell fashioned himself as a man that knew livestock. He'd looked here, there, and everywhere for a mule to replace his that had died back in the winter. It was springtime and no one had a horse, mule, or steer for sale that would suit him.

One Sunday as we stood around the stove in the meetinghouse, Strubbs brought up news about a mule. "I hear tell Will Gorman has a young mule that stands eighteen hands high."

"Are you sure?" I asked. "I hadn't heard Calvin say a thing about having a good mule like that."

Strubbs didn't like folks to ask him questions; he spoke right up. "I am. That's my kind of stock-- I hear he looks the best--long-legged with sound feet and teeth."

He seemed to put a lot of thought in how it looked, but nothing about how it worked or rode.

Strubbs went right on, like he was talking over my head. "I need an outstanding mule to replace Big Red, my good mule that died a while back."

Everyone in the church knew that Big Red had been wind-broke. Strubbs had to sprinkle water and mineral oil on its hay so the poor mule could get its breath. Most of the men tried to hint to him that any stock Will Gorman had that late in the season had something bad wrong with it.

"I'd be a'studyin on it before I'd buy this time of year from Will," Albert Sizemore said.

"Amen," Reverend Laban said. "That's clear as spring water."

"Well," Strubbs said, "I know more about stock than any of you."

I was over at the Gorman's place a week or so later when Strubbs came walking up. He'd got a For-Hire to bring him. A thunderstorm had made the road so bad the little truck couldn't make it all the way. Strubbs had to walk from Footers.

"I've come to trade on the big young mule," Strubbs said, right off. "That truck driver is the poorest hand to drive I've ever witnessed."

"Calvin!" Will said. "Go fetch the black mule out."

"Why don't you work with this mule any?" I said as we led the critter back toward the house.

"He's a plug, all looks and nothing else."

Strubbs did most of the talking as the big black mule pranced around him. "I know a lot about mules, and this'n here is a dandy--you cain't fool me when it comes to livestock."

Even I noticed there was no sign of where the mule had worn a collar or gears--no marks of where trace chains or singletrees had rubbed its legs.

Strubbs talked about how he could tell a mule's age to within a month and cure any ailment that's ever been in livestock. I had to smile. Everybody in these parts came to Will Gorman when they had sick stock, even the veterinarian from over in Asheville.

"How's the mule pull?" Strubbs said.

I was tickled that he got around to the thing that mattered. I'm sure Dad would have asked that first.

"When you get to the foot of a hill, he's right there," Will said.

It was as plain as the feathers on a goose that Strubbs meant to have the mule. Ever since he got there, Strubbs had eyed a red buggy that belonged to Calvin.

"Us both being good traders," Strubbs said to Will, "I'll make it a hundred and fifty dollars if you'll throw in the buggy."

"Son," Will said, when Strubbs led the mule out around the pasture, "that's a lot of money he's offering. If you want to let it go, I'll give you the hundred and I'll keep the fifty for the mule."

A deal was struck.

"It's usually hard for two traders to trade this fast," Strubbs said, when he got back. "Reckon it goes to show how much we both know about stock."

Strubbs hooked up the mule to the buggy and headed off down the road. Along late in the evening he came walking back up leading the mule without the buggy. It was plain by the mule's hide that Strubbs had used many a tree limb on him. I knew that wouldn't set well with Will Gorman.

"When we got down off this mountain and started up Rocky Meadows," Strubbs said, "this mule wouldn't even pull up through Walnut Flats. I want my money back. You said this mule would pull."

"Not so," Will said. "I told you that when you got to the foot of a hill, he'd be right there. Well, right there is where he's going to stay if he's hooked to anything."

It was plain as the nose on the mule that Strubbs liked its looks so much that he wanted to keep it. Will, he tried to reason with Strubbs and even offered to take the mule to Georgia and sell it. Strubbs wouldn't hear of it, even though he knew he would get every penny the mule brought. Will offered Strubbs his money back if the buggy wasn't hurt. Strubbs wouldn't even hear to that. An hour later, Will agreed to trade him a saddle for the buggy. Calvin went to the barn and brought back an old McClelland army saddle.

When it was all said and done, Will got the worth out of the mule and Calvin sold a five-dollar saddle for a hundred bucks.

Strubbs kept the mule for a couple of years. He sold it to a drummer who got from place to place on mule-back.

Dad hadn't made mention of the pin-hookers in quite a spell. I figured as how they weren't such a worry to him, else folks got wise and run them off.

"We're leaving early in the morning," Dad said one day while we split locust fence posts. "Gonna take the posts and sell them."

We parked under the big oak tree on the square, a full mile from the cattle sale. There wasn't a soul in sight.

"How're we going to sell the posts?" I said. "Farmers will all be down yonder at the sale barn."

Dad didn't answer, so I wondered if the posts were just a put-on to come to the sale when we didn't have anything else to sell.

I forgot all about the posts, anyway, when Will and Calvin drove up and parked their truck. They didn't have any livestock with them, either.

Calvin climbed up on the posts beside me. We talked, but I couldn't figure out what we were doing there. There were no people to buy our posts, nor any stock for Will to look at.

A little later, an old farmer drove up with a cow and calf in a truck. Dad and Will climbed up on the truck for a look.

"My lord, they've done took up pin-hooking," I said, loud enough for Dad to hear.

"Just you watch," Dad said.

I watched close.

It came to me that they'd picked a time when all the pin-hookers would be back. Folks would be selling all the stock they didn't have winter feed for.

"Ernest, we figure the cow and calf ought to fetch close to seventy-five dollars," Will said.

A few minutes later a man with two steers drove up; Dad turned to Will. "What do you think?"

Black'n will go right at a thousand, the whiteface a right smart more. I'd say eleven-thirty to eleven thirty-five.

Dad handed the man a piece of notebook paper with some writing that looked like Mama's hand. "This is the price quoted in the paper yesterday."

Will and Dad kept it up all morning, sizing up the cattle that went to the sale. They seemed to be having a good time.

We left for the sale a few minutes before it was to start. Calvin sat beside me on the posts as we rode toward the sale barn.

"Them pin-hookers don't look none too happy," I said as we passed the men milling around the front of the barn.

Calvin laughed. "Their faces are as long as some of these fence posts."

As the sale went along, the farmers' faces seemed to brighten up. The packinghouse buyers didn't wipe their faces every minute. The pin-hookers had to work like the devil to break even.

Dad seemed well pleased on the ride home that night, although we hadn't sold a post.

"It don't differ," he said. "We had us a good day."

The next month he went by himself to the sale. I stayed home and helped Mama can the hog we had killed the day before.

"You're so happy, a body would of thought you'd come into money," Mama said, when Dad got home.

He laughed til it looked like his sides hurt.

"Where's the pin-hookers?" I said the next month as we turned off the road to the sale barn.

They won't be back, Dad said. Told McAllen they couldn't make gas money around here for some reason.

TEACHER -- Starting Out With a Lie

Dad and Mama went at it every time he stopped plowing to catch his breath. He sat down behind the plow and rested while we caught up with the hoeing. Once Mama got within earshot, they started.

He slung the half-full gourd of water across the patch. "Who is this girl-woman that you let move into the empty house down the road?"

"Her name is Mattie. She's a Starns."

"I know of her. She's pert-near twenty-five years old. I saw her in town this Saturday past."

"She's been a'sparkin Wait Nations. He'd do hisself proud if'n he'd hitch up with her."

"Wait, let's see--that's old Snake Nations' boy, from over on Vengeance Creek."

"The same; he'd do good to marry her. She's a fine girl. And a looker, too."

"She's with--I mean, Waits a decent sort. She won't pull double with that man." Dad stood up and hung the check lines around his neck. We'll talk more about it back at the house. Git up there, Sally."

"Hush up that kind of talk," Mama said. "Aunt Airenell Patton said Mattie would make a good school marm; she'd show her how. Airenell ought to know. She's taught over a thousand little'uns all over these here mountains."

By then, Dad was fifty feet away. I heard him mumbling as he went out the row. "Gee. Another one coming on. Gee there. I never figured out that Airenell woman either. Gee. Gee, come up, dang you Sally, you're getting contrarier'n hell--just like'em."

I'd heard that Mama let somebody move into the empty house a week ago yesterday, but I hadn't inquired who it was. Mama took in every stray that came by. Anybody or anything with a sad look or sad story got the run of the place. I knew Wait Nations better than any of them did. He owned a little mule. He plowed for folks all summer and skidded pole wood all winter. Sometimes he let me and Ceece help. Wait was slim and tan from all the hard work, and his hair was yellow from going bareheaded in the sun. He seemed to be about seven or eight years older than me; that would put him in his middle to late twenties.

The last schoolteacher we had was old man Cebe Mullins. He had stayed at our school a time and a time. He came so long ago you'd have to be old to remember. Folks said he came right after the

Airenell woman went to Cades Cove. His beard reached all the way down to his belt.

"What do you think of this Mattie?" I said to Reek, who helped hoe the corn and was out of earshot of either Dad or Mama. "Dad don't think much of her."

Reek, he loaded his lip with snuff like he was about to spit out a bunch of words. Then he picked up a piece of locust root about six inches long and started to whittle.

I wished I hadn't asked. Reek didn't deal with any women except Mama and then only when he was eating her cooking. He knew to take that old hat off and wash up and bow his head when grace was said. Again, I wished I hadn't asked. "I'm going down to the spring to get me a drink of fresh water," I said and took off toward the spring, jumping over two rows at a time.

I got me a drink and walked back to the corn patch. "Everybody knew Mr. Mullins was leaving," Mama said to one of my older sisters. "Going back to be buried where he was raised over in Polk County."

Our school was over on Hiwassee River about twenty some-odd miles from town. Ceece, all my sisters and me were the only ones from Rail Cove that walked across the ridge every day when school was going on. Mama saw to it that we went.

All in all, there was about seventeen that went regular. The schoolhouse sat on a little rise between two big white oak trees in the bend of the river. The building was older than time and hard to heat. It must have been built as a school for it don't have any kitchen or parlor; looked something like a church, but it was way to little to have meetings in. There was talk of them running a bus up this way in a year or two and we would go into town to school. To costly and hard to get teachers to come this far back in the mountains, the county claimed.

I heard a rain crow squawk like they do in the fall. It wouldn't be long before school started again. Besides that, Shirley Ammons had the prettiest black hair you about ever seen. She was two years older than me and hadn't give me any reason to get my hopes up. I'd have walked her home in a minute, if'n she'd let me.

Dad finished plowing and drove Sally toward the barn. Mama pointed her hoe up the hillside. "You finish hoeing that last five rows, I'm going to the house and can some beans before I have to get supper. And make sure you get the morning glories off them down in the hollow."

"I'll go down and see this Mattie when I get done." I had to be talking to myself. Every body else was twenty rows away with their backs turned. "I'll figure out what Dad is talking about."

It took me the balance of the evening to work out the few rows. The blamed morning glories wrapped around the corn stalks like hay bailing wire. I quit talking to myself and jerked the last few vines off, stripping the corn stalks bare.

It was near dusky dark when I got to the foot-log leading over to the house where this Mattie lived. When I got halfway across, I saw her come out the kitchen door with a wash-pan full of soapy water. She poured it on some wilted-looking roses. I stopped and stood still so's she wouldn't see me and get scared.

She was right pretty. Her black hair shined even in the dim light. I generally didn't pay much mind to how girls were built, cause it was all them older sisters of mine had on their minds. They talked about being round in the right places. Most of the time they just stood around waiting for some parts to grow. Under the green dress this Mattie wore, it looked like her body was filled out pretty well. Her eyes were not exactly blue. Their color put me in mind of a young saw briar vine. Everybody in our family and most of the ones we knew had black eyes. Maybe they was what Dad didn't like about her.

She was not as pretty as the girl that I had tried to take up with down at the mill. Anyway, this Mattie was pert-near ten years older than me, according to Dad. Girls were sorta like horses; sometimes I liked'em and sometimes I didn't. I hoped she didn't talk as much as my younger sisters or pester everybody to death like Ceece did.

After she went back in the house, I sat down on a big rock and tried to whittle something out of a laurel stick. That didn't work, so I whetted my knife on a piece of sandstone for a while.

A little later I got my nerve up and went to the door. "My name's Quill, Quill Vance."

"I know, your sisters told me. I've been here going on a week. I didn't have much to move, as you can see."

Her voice was low and clear. Inside by the coal oil lamp she was prettier than she looked outside.

"Hugggh, huggh." I cleared my throat. "I came down to see if I could help you out--maybe cut wood or move something."

"Wait brought me enough wood to last a spell. You can help me move the bedstead. Wait made it out of green lumber and it weighs a ton."

It took both of us on one end to walk the thing over against the far wall. She gave me some cookies and a snuff glass full of tea. The cookies were hard as a brick but the tea was sweet. I wallowed the whole thing around in my mouth until I could swallow it.

A while later, I left for home, hoping her and Wait would get married and live here a long time. Up to then I couldn't figure out anything about what Dad was trying to say. Maybe he wasn't as good a judge of women as he was when he married Mama. She sure had a better way about her than my sisters did.

Things went along about like you'd suspect. Wait came down the road by the house every evening along about dark. Even if I didn't see him, I could tell by the way that his left foot slapped the ground. One Saturday he bought enough walnut lumber from Dad's stack in the barn to make a fitting bed.

Ceece wanted to do something to scare Wait, as was a common practice hereabouts when folks knew a man was sparking a woman like Wait was. "We could jump out at him as he rounds that dark curve. Use a bed sheet and holler like a river panther."

"I'll have no part of it," I said. "You're afraid of your shadow after dark. You won't go nowhere after dark without a torchlight of some kind."

"Yeah, the reason is, you done took up sparkin the girls. I seed you kiss and rub around on that girl down at the picture show a week-ago Saturday. And I seed the tickle and grin you and that girl was a'doin out behind the mill."

That nosy thing knew every move I made. "You tell a soul," I said, "and I'll leave you some night in the darkest place I can find--you hear me?"

"Well, hell fire, forget I brought it up."

School started on the first day of September. With the three Straton girls from Wolf Creek we had twenty starting. That Hansi Straton was one fine figure of a girl. Her older sisters didn't look quite as good, but they were no slouches neither. My sisters' eyes popped out when Hansi walked by. The best part was, she was my age. She had brown hair that curled like the waves on water, eyes that shined like marbles, and teeth that sparkled like ice in the sunshine. I looked at the papers on the teacher's desk; I was only two days older than she was. School was about to become my favorite place.

The county school people sent word that they were coming to talk about our school. They came on Monday two weeks after school commenced and called a meeting at the schoolhouse late that evening.

They started right in and questioned the fact that some of the kids going to our school lived in Wolf Creek. It was a ways over in Georgia. Some others lived in Cades Cove over in Tennessee. Our school was ten miles closer to them than any in their states.

When they had their say, Dad got up. "We'll run this part, you run yours. Every since time beginst we've ran our school here in the cove. Took up subscriptions and hired our own teachers and such. Two years ago you said you wanted to help, when what you wanted was to run the place." Dad's face tuned a little red and I knew he wasn't through yet. "You let us say what's what about our school. Now you take this place where we live. You can stand with one foot in one state and put the other foot in another. At the same time you can piss in another." Dad didn't normally say that much, but he sent the county people packing.

"You come on pretty strong with them county officials," Mama said as we rode home in our truck.

"I had it to do," was all Dad said.

It was along about the first hard freeze when two men came to the school house door. They looked to be around twenty years old. From their looks and the clothes they wore, they had to be brothers. Both wore their hats cocked to the left, almost covering their eye.

Mattie held the door open and the tallest one stood in front of her. He pulled his hat off and held it in his right hand. "Scuse me teacher woman, do you have any girls here?"

"We have several. Why do you ask?"

"I mean, are any of them of marring age?"

I could see that I was about to loose my chance with Hansi. She was by far the prettiest one there.

"No," Mattie said and shut the door.

All day long we saw the men sitting under one of the white oak trees. The older girls saw them too, for they were forever walking back and forth by the window like they had to sharpen their pencils.

When school let out the men met the girls at the door. I thought Mattie was going to have a running fit. She muttered under her breath something that I made out to be: "Men drive me crazy."

I was about to ask her what she meant, but Ceece ran over to me. "They's a'leavin with them old Rose sisters."

"Who is?"

"Why, them men."

We watched as the four of them walked the path leading over to the cove where the girls lived. The Rose sisters were a year older than any of the other girls. They were a stocky-built pair that hardly ever spoke. All I knew about any of the Rose clan is, every last one of the men made a living splitting out clapboards for roofs.

"Do you think they'll marry up with them old Rose girls?" Ceece said before we got to the top of the ridge on our way home.

I hoped they would take them Rose sisters. If not, they might try to take Hansi off. It wouldn't be until after the fight. I never let on to Ceece or my sisters about how I felt.

The next day went the same. The men showed up shortly after we had our diner break and sat under the white oak. Strangest thing that happened was how all the girls carried on. Some of them painted their lips and cheeks with bee's wax that they had died red. My youngest sister looked like she had poke berry juice smeared around her mouth, from ear to ear. They giggled and carried on until I even forgot to look at Hansi every chance I got.

The only one of the Simon girls that had blue-green eyes rubbed dog thistle in her eyes to make the center larger so's she looked to have black eyes. Ceece talked me into doing it once even though we already had black eyes. The centers got so big that the sunlight hurt like fire.

Mattie worried me most. She didn't act like the others, more like she hated them men. For a flat week, every day was the same. The men came--the girls acted crazy. They wouldn't talk to us boys. They huddled to themselves and if I heard the words "Spin the bottle" one time, I heard them a hundred.

The following Monday the Rose sisters didn't show up at school. The girls all whispered to themselves until Mattie walked up in front. "The Rose sisters left with the two young men for West Virginia."

The jabbering flew. It was another week before the girls started acting like they had one lick of sense.

Ever since I learned to drive, one or more of my sisters would come around acting so sweet butter wouldn't melt in their mouths. "Teach me to drive."

"There ain't one drop of gas in the truck," I said, "ain't been since last week."

They didn't understand, or else they didn't care, for an hour later some of them would ask again. Then one allowed. "Put some lamp oil in the cussed thing. It burns."

"Dad would tan my hide good."

"Well, walk over to the mill and buy some."

"I've got to go see Reek." I went toward the cove road.

If it wasn't my sisters, it was Reek worrying me about going somewhere. I didn't want to see Reek, for all he did was come down every evening and talk like he had a great secret. "Shaw, I know where the biggest buck that ever walked on four legs is. I seed his track." The first break in the cold weather he done the same. "Shaw, there's a rainbow trout in that deep hole over in the Nantahala River that's over two feet long. I hooked on to him a week ago Friday."

"Reek, there ain't no less than a thousand deep holes in that river."

"Shaw, I recollect it was a week ago Friday."

He wasn't about to let me know where the fish was, or the deer, for that matter. I went to the woods with him three or four times a week.

Winter was about to set in and I hadn't walked Hansi home one blessed time. I'd brought her chinquapins every fall for three straight years. She loved the sweet little chestnut-like nuts; so did every one of the other girls. The way they acted, I couldn't give the nuts to any of them. At least I didn't have to save the best ones. It about made me sick, I ate so many.

Monday morning I had every pocket of my overalls stuffed, and both side pockets of my coat. I held out two hands full in front of the girls. "Do you want any chinquapins?" They all looked at me as if I was trying to give them rotten eggs or something. I flew mad, walked to the wood stove, and threw every last one of them in the firebox. The girls' eyes got big as saucers, but they didn't utter a sound.

Wait spent more time down at Mattie's since the only work he had for himself and the mule was snaking pole wood for people to use for heat.

It started to bother Mama some that there were no weddings plans being made. One evening, as I ate a late supper, Mama sat down beside Dad and lit in. "Do you know if he has asked her? What in this world is he waiting on?"

"Who asked who what?" Dad said.

"You know blame good and well I'm talking about Wait and Mattie. He don't show much spunk. If'n he did, there'd be wedding plans to attend to."

Dad moved around the table and sat down beside me. He had a look on his face that put me in mind of how a dog looked that had been caught sucking eggs.

"I ain't got no idea," I said.

"Find out," Mama went. "I want to help them. And wipe them smirks off your Dad's face."

"I'll try and find out," I said, "but I got no idea how."

Dad sipped his coffee as if somehow he'd gone deaf. Why was Mama so dead-set on marring them off and Dad so against it? It puzzled me. Was it because she was a woman teacher? That didn't fit Dad's way of thinking a'tall. I couldn't reason out that it had anything to do with her age, him being so strict on letting my older sisters court and all. It seemed to suit him if they didn't get married until they were in their fifties. The way they acted, nobody but a crazy person would marry them anyhow.

While I was walking down the road to Mattie's, I pondered what Mama had said. Better still, I could ask Wait--he didn't talk much. I could ask Mattie, but she was a woman and might tell me to mind my own affairs.

By the time I got to the foot log, I heard Wait's foot slapping the ground behind me. I looked back for he hadn't come around the curve yet.

I walked right on by the foot log leading to Mattie's and hurried on down the road. The reason, if there was one, was so Wait and Mattie could be alone for a spell. Anyhow, I never let up until I got to the mouth of the cove where the road forks. There was a big flint rock, and I sat down for the better part of an hour. Would the fact that Mattie was a Starns have anything to do with the way Dad felt about her?

At full dark, I guessed the thing to do was go back up the road and tell Mama I hadn't found out anything. I'd been gone for over an hour--she'd think I tried.

Going by the house where Mattie lived, I tried to walk in the worn places and on flat rocks so her and Wait wouldn't hear me. Just when I got even with the foot log, I saw Wait standing on the bottom step and Mattie in the doorway. Neither said anything at first, then Wait's voice started out low. "Mattie, what in tarnation are you telling me. You have been--oh hell, you're still married."

"That's what I've been trying to tell you. Wait, at least try to understand."

"Hell, it ain't hard, you're a married woman."

"Please try to understand."

"Do you have any more tricks about you?"

"What do you mean? Won't you please try to understand?"

"You cain't pass your self off as a virgin now, can you?"

"Wait, try to understand."

"Dam it to hell." Wait started toward the foot log. I broke into a dead run, not wanting him to know what I had heard.

"It was my folks' idea that I marry him," Mattie said. "His family had money."

A body couldn't fault Wait for being mad. I wanted to talk to him and see if I could do something. Down deep, I knew there was nothing. If I tried it would make matters worse. Maybe he wouldn't take it so hard after he slept on it. And no way in blazes could I come up with any idea. The sound of his footsteps went by our house fifteen minutes later.

I sat at the table and drank the stale coffee left over from supper. As my sisters got older, Mama and them talked about things like that from time to time.

I recalled last Thursday night. They were all sitting around the table, each one hoping the others would start clearing the supper dished, I figured. Mama had me over in the corner working--doing the bookwork Mattie had sent home with me.

"I'm here to tell you," my younger sister allowed, "when my time comes, I'm a'gonna marry me a rich man."

"You better marry for love," Mama said, "not for money or position."

"Why?" the next youngest said. "I know what you always say: don't try to get above your raisin."

"Money and position are like walking on stilts," Mama said. "All you can do is fall off. On the other hand, love is like glue; it can hold people together year after year."

"It's as easy to love a rich man as it is a poor'un," the youngest sister fired back.

"No body goin to marry her no-how," I said, gathering up my papers and heading for another room.

Them matters of love and stuff was harder to figure out than anything I'd come up against. Getting older sure didn't make things easier. Anyway, I wasn't going to think on it no more right then. A night bird flew against the kitchen door and brought me back to my mind.

After that, the house was quiet, and by the fourth cup, my head sank onto the table. All night, thoughts fluttered through my head like butterflies.

Sometime during the night, I must have wandered to my bed, for Mama came to get me up a little after daylight. "Your Dad and Reek have gone to work on the water line. They'll be looking for you to help."

I jumped up and ran through the house. It was Saturday and I wanted to get out of the house before she set in on me about Mattie and Wait.

We'd had water in the house for some time and Dad was forever running the line farther up the branch. "If we only go to the next spring, higher up, we'll have a site more pressure," he said, four or five times, the day before.

"We have enough pressure that you have to have a death grip on a glass when you turn on the spigot, else it'll knock it out of your hand and break it," Mama said.

"Why don't you take up dipping snuff, then we'll have plenty of drinking glasses."

Mama grabbed up an armload of corn and went into the house.

There was no way we could bury the pipe in the boulder field the branch runs through. So we had to lay it in the branch making sure it was covered with water, so as not to freeze come winter. By the time I got there, all I could see of Dad and Reek were their heads. They had scratched out a flat place to lay the pipe and had rolled boulders against it. Each rock was laid just so--to keep the pipe from bending.

Dad looked up at me. "What kept you?"

I jumped down in the spring branch without answering. After every hard winter rain I would have to climb farther to check the pipe, so it behooved me to fix it the best I could.

I dodged around, once we finished, to see if Wait went by. Mostly, I wanted to stay away from the house and Mama. At full dark, Wait hadn't passed, and I heard Mama and my sisters putting together their things to wear to church the next morning. Long after the ruckus died down I slipped into the house and went to bed.

Sunday morning it wasn't hard to stay out of the way. My sisters argued about everything they had to wear and who would be looking and such as that. It was one clash after another and it kept Mama busy. When it was all said, they looked as good as they could, taking into account what they had to work with. Anyway, when it came time to leave, they acted like little angles, smiling and carrying on as if they had never had a cross word.

Mattie didn't show her face at church, and I was glad. I thought that maybe she went to another church. Heck, I knew better. I pinched my arm for telling myself lies.

Late in the evening I sat down by the corncrib and watched for Wait. He never passed. Again it was easy to slip into the house and to bed without Mama saying anything to me.

That Monday at school Mattie looked haggard. She was a good teacher even with all the worry. I tried my best not to let on that I knew anything. Every time I had thoughts of my sisters and the other girls at school finding out, I got cold chills

After supper, Mama called me off to herself, out near the wood shed. "What do you know about Wait and Mattie? He's stopped going down there."

"I don't have no notion; couldn't find out nothing."

"Did you ask? I mean, didn't you hear them talking?"

"I heard them talking, but they weren't planning on no marryin, I don't think." I figured she was about to call my hand and ask what it was I heard.

"Well," she said, "I hate to keep on about it. Just listen and watch, will you. Six or seven people asked me the same question at church."

"Yes Ma'am," I said. I hadn't heard one word spoke about it at church but I knew them older folks talked. They'd ask some simple questions that didn't sound like they meant anything, yet when it was all said and done it meant everything. Because Mattie lived so close to us is the reason they asked Mama, I reckon.

Them folks wouldn't hold to a married woman courting--for sure not a schoolteacher. If it were a man they would ride him out on a rail, or else tar and feather him.

Time passed and I didn't go down the road to Mattie's much any more. I didn't want to face her, knowing what I did. Wait never walked by the house again. Mattie did her job as a teacher and carried the rent money to Mama as regular as clockwork. She would come near dark and wouldn't say a half dozen words.

"Does Mattie stay in her house?" Mama said, one evening when I came into the kitchen with an armload of stove wood.

"Don't know any more than a barn door." I dropped the wood and looked around to see if Aunt Nica or any of my sisters was near. There was no one else in that part of the house. I felt like I was going to be put on the spot.

"I've got a feeling she's not staying there," Mama said, "that's all."

After supper I finished feeding the stock and wandered down the road without letting anyone know. I didn't care much for this spying and this way I was the only one who knew if I found out anything.

Mattie's house was dark and nobody had walked near the doorstep since it rained three days before. There was no need in calling so I went back by the barn and picked up the eggs and went home. I thought that maybe she was living up the cove with Wait. That couldn't have been so or else she would have to pass our house on the way to school. I remembered the quilts I saw rolled up in the back of the school. Were they there in case there was a big snow and Mattie had to stay over? Had she been sleeping in the school? Was that why she looked so bad? I thought of what Mama had said after Mattie paid the rent. "She's falling off. I don't think she's eating right."

That was like a puzzle where the more you found out, the further you were from the answer.

It all broke at once. Word came that the county officials were visiting again the next Friday, and Mama told Dad, "Tonight we need to straighten this mess out so we'll at least know how to answer them."

"How do you know they're coming on account of Mattie?" Dad said.

"They know she is a married woman."

Dad set his coffee cup down. "Pregnant too?"

"What makes you think that?"

"I saw her in town, and I can tell."

"Where did you get to be an authority on pregnant women?"

"From you. All pregnant women look the picture of health when they've been that way a couple of months. Look like they are wearing lip rouge all over their face, when they're not."

"So, you're telling me we don't have a chance?"

"Woman, you're the kind that if a body finds themselves in some kind of a fix you'll stay with them, come hell or high water."

"You will at least go to the meeting, won't you?"

I sure hoped he would, for if Mama got started the first thing that would happen was, her chin would quiver. The next thing, she'd break out crying; after that, she'd stop crying and light in on them with words they hadn't never heard.

"I've got business in town that day," Dad said. "You can read their title clear. I've heard you."

I dodged around the balance of the week and wouldn't even talk to the others at school about Mattie--or the county people that were coming. I did watch and listen for Wait to go down the road late in the evening but he never did.

Dad left out before daybreak Friday morning and was gone before any of us knew it. He had it figured out at the onset and Mama wouldn't listen; no wonder he slipped out early. Still and all, the least he could do was go and hold Mama's hand and offer to do what he could.

There were half again as many county people there as before, and some were great big men. Every grownup from Lick Rock to Frog Mountain filled the room. Many were way too old to have kids in school. Even my uncles from all the way over on the Pigeon River at Sugarland sat against the south wall. I figured they must have traveled the better part of that day.

"My lord," Mama said, "there're flocking in here like a bunch of guineas in a field of grasshoppers."

I sat up front near the teacher's desk where I always had. Mama claimed it was the place where she sat when she went to school, but I figured she just wanted me right under the teacher's nose.

The meeting got started at 7 o'clock. I looked for Dad but he wasn't there. Wait hadn't bothered to come either.

A man from the county rose and walked to the stand where Mattie taught us kids. "The meeting

47

will be called to order. There is only one item on our agenda, so we can dispense with anything other than the matter at hand. The teacher's deplorable behavior."

Some of the words didn't make a lot of sense to me. At first, I didn't understand, but everybody there knew Mattie was who it was all about. It looked like them folks from the county had brought all their big guns and were ready to tell my folks what was what. They even brought a state man from some way-off place, like Asheville.

I wasn't paying much mind. I tried to see if there was anyone my age in the crowd. If the truth be known, I was looking for Hansi. Anyway, the state man looked like an over-fed bulldog. I did hear'em say, "the state man will set them straight later on."

The county man cleared his throat and went right on. "It is a long way to town and we need to leave soon. We will follow the standard rules of order and if you don't know what they are refrain from speaking, in other words, keep quiet."

Mattie had taught us about the rules of order just the week before, but I was sure the older folks didn't know what they are all about. Mountain folks had a way of speaking their minds when they were good and ready.

I looked at the door. Where was Dad? He never cared what happened to Mattie or else he'd be here to say his piece. If him and Reek went off dog trading, I'd give him a piece of my mind when I saw him even if he did give me a whuping. Mama looked like she'd lost her last friend. Her black eyes looked like wet chestnuts. I started twice to ask her were in the hell Dad was. Both times, I didn't have the heart to make it any worse for her.

Another man rose when the first fellow sat back down. "The woman in question is not present, I see. Her father, a friend of mine, married the rest of his girls to outstanding young men from the city."

I looked over my right shoulder and there sat Aunt Nica and my oldest two sisters, big as life. Mama left her to look after my sisters. What was Aunt Nica doing here? She wouldn't know about anything other than cooking, canning and cleaning. She called courting a fool's playground. If Aunt Nica took up the cause she would give them their come-up'ns; her tongue's sharper than a new tobacco knife.

Down at church last spring a woman slapped a little boy for crying. She was a big woman--nearly six feet tall, and she must have weighed two hundred pounds. Aunt Nica wasn't more'n five feet, and Dad would say she's no bigger than a bar of soap after a week's washing. It didn't matter-- Aunt Nica was right up in the woman's face as quick as a cat. "You beanie-eyed bitch, come outside. I intend to pull out every hair on that empty hat rack you call a head." It took Dad and

Mama both--one on each of Aunt Nica's arms--to lead her away from the church. They couldn't turn loose until we were halfway up the cove.

Mama's chin started to quiver. She bit her lip to make it stop. A tear ran down her left cheek. I reached into my pocket for something to wipe it with. I wished I had stayed at home. Where was Dad? Why wasn't he there? Where--

Behind, me some women took their text out on Wait. "Where is that trifling Wait?" A low voice said.

"You cain't put no dependence in the likes of him," a little louder voice said.

"We all know the baby ain't his'n," a loud voice joined in. "He don't have no backbone. He couldn't raise a fever in a cat's rear-end."

The door flew open as if a strong wind had come up. My head spun around like an owl's.

Dad walked into the schoolhouse with his hat held out in front of him like he was taking up the offering at church. By the time he got halfway down the isle, his jaw was set and his teeth were clinched. Mattie held onto his right arm, her head down toward her feet. It put me in mind of leading a calf to slaughter. Nobody spoke to them as they made their way to the front. You could have heard a marble roll across the floor.

Dad dropped his hat onto the teacher's desk. Rocks the size of eggs bounced out of his hat and it sounded like he'd hit the desk with a hammer.

Dad's jaws worked slowly open. "I've come to say my piece. We all know what's going on here. I know we have young folks in our midst. Well, there ain't a kid over five in these mountains that's not seen sex taking place between animals and know all about where babies come from. We're here to see if civilized people can have the same respect and act toward each other at least as well as critters do."

"You are out of order!" A big man from town got out of his chair.

Dad picked up the hat full of rocks, walked right up in the man's face and held out the hat. "So you want to be the one to cast the first stone?"

The man's face got as white as the first snowflakes of winter. Dad stared at him like an eagle. Dad's black eyes darted from the man to the prettiest one of the women from the county--like he was talking to her too. A minute later the man wilted back down into his chair.

Dad went right back to talking as he offered each county official the rocks. "Me and Mattie just came from the lawyers office and the divorce papers have been filed. Her only offense, or sin, if you wish, was listening to somebody trying to live her life for her. The right thing to do, Ladies and Gentlemen, is for us to show our support. Me and mine intend to do just that. She can teach out this year and have the baby next summer. We'll help raise it if need be. Lord, how could one more matter?"

"No you won't." Wait's voice came from back in the room. "I plan to hitch up with Mattie once the divorce comes through. We'll raise the young'un. It won't be no orphan or called a bastard if we have to move all the way to Calif--"

He was cut short by two of our neighbors that jumped to their feet. Mr. Hawkins, the oldest, didn't mince his words. "That settles it in my mind. A bunch that won't look after their own don't need schools no how. We ain't gonna act like no heathens. What do the rest of you say?"

I waited for the state man to say something. I guess he was scared, being this far back in the mountains.

Ever last person got to their feet, even one lady that came with the county people.

The man that seemed to be the leader rose ever so slow. "I guess it's settled. We'll see how it works out."

Almost to a person, they nodded their heads. They started talking about the weather and hog killing.

I looked around and saw Wait standing against the north wall. He had on a grin that ran all the way across his face. Mama reached out and took Dad's hand, even where everybody could see. They stood

52

around and talked way into the night like a big family. Neither the officials nor anyone else spoke a word about what they came here for.

I felt someone take hold of my right hand. "Walk me home," Hansi said.

SPECK -- Young Dog, Old Tricks

"Hyar! Hyar! Hyar!" Dad waded into the pack of fighting dogs.

He knocked them right and left--he kicked one lanky hound so hard it turned three somersaults and landed in the garden on its back. The dog let out a long yelp and returned to the fight.

Most people who kept hunting dogs tied them up along the creek bank. Each one had its own shelter, usually a rusty barrel, with the end cut out. Our dogs ran loose. They slept together in the truck shed, except when one was in season. Then we'd put her up in the loft of the corncrib. You could always tell when we did. The others barked all blamed night long.

A dogfight was something that took place every day. This one only lasted a few minutes. There wasn't much blood on the ground. None were hurt bad. Dad had won, as usual. Each of the twenty dogs took off in a different direction. All except

Ol' Lead. He came up from the branch, showed his fangs, and growled. Dad hit him between the eyes with a tobacco stick. The hound turned and took off down the road with his tail all the way between his legs, yelping with every jump.

"Ol' Lead's one of the best huntin dogs I ever seen, but he don't have quittin sense." Dad dropped the tobacco stick back on the pile.

The fight ended. Every dog but Ol' Lead came to Dad to get some petting.

"Keepin dogs tied up makes their feet tender," Dad said that night as we sat on the porch with our neighbor Reek Moore.

"Shaw," Reek said. "For a fact, their toenails get so long they cain't run. A body can lose a whole huntin season while their nails wear off and their feet toughen up."

Reek was a bachelor man that lived just up the cove a'ways. He came down to our house every night, either to go hunting or fishing, or to make plans to do one or the other. Reek was getting on in years. It troubled Mama some that Reek didn't know how old he was and things like that. He had high cheekbones and what Mama called a Roman nose.

"He's bald as a pumpkin," my little sister said, ever time anybody brought up talk about Reek.

That night Mama jumped him again. "Reek, How old are you? Do you have any close kin living? Don't give me another date for when you were born unless you know for sure."

"Shaw, I don't rightly know. The Bible burned right after my Ma died."

"Don't you recall the names and dates?"

"Shaw no. That ain't nothin to fret about. A body lives til his time comes.

"Well I hate to keep asking," Mama said. I'd--.

That's about the size of it." Dad brought it to a stop. "Reek knows every branch, hollow, cove, trail, and bear den, and where every good stand of mast trees is within fifty miles of Rail Cove. He don't have time for such foolishness as when he was born or who his kin are."

"Shaw, shaw." Reek said. That thar's a fact."

"Well," Mama said, "it matters to some."

Dad spoke up. "We need to see if we can replace that dog we lost last year in the Nantahala Gorge. Huntin season is right now on us."

"Shaw yes, he was a good-un," Reek said, and all but choked on snuff as he spoke. "I hate that he fell off that thar cliff and got kilt."

Mama got out of her chair and went toward the garden. "Everybody knows you cain't get a word in edge-wise when they talk about dogs and huntin."

"There's a Preacher over in Sottowag," Dad said. "I hear tell he's got him a good stock of dogs."

"Shaw. Shaw. Plotts, Black and Tans, Treein Walkers--they all good dogs." Reek flipped the snuff out of his mouth with his finger.

"I have always been partial to mixed breeds." Dad rubbed his right hand through his beard. "Pure breeds sometimes have a peculiarity I don't like."

"Shaw. I never put much stock in how dogs are marked, neither."

That settled it. The next morning Dad, Reek, and I headed out for the Sottowag Community. Reek talked like a little kid going after some candy. It took the better part of the morning to cross over Hothouse Ridge into Taylor County.

Dad stopped the truck at a fork in the road. A short, stooping man was chopping corn stalks and throwing them across a fence to a milk cow.

"I hear tell there's a preacher here-abouts who's got huntin dogs to sell," Dad said.

"Jist follow the road up that thar cove a ways," the old man said. "You cain't miss the place. Hit's covered up with blamed dogs."

"Shaw. Shaw. It looks like a dog farm," Reek said, when we drove up in the yard.

There were dogs tied to every tree on the hillside, they barked like crazy. I started to count, but lost it at forty-seven.

The preacher came out on the porch before Dad had stopped the truck. He was tall and thin, and he had the longest white beard I had ever seen. A black frock coat hung from his shoulders to the top of his dirty boots--a flat-brimmed felt hat almost covered his eyes.

"What do you want?" the preacher asked. His Adam's apple bounced up and down behind the backward collar and beard.

"Come to see about buyin a dog," Dad said.

"I don't put no price on a dog's head," the preacher said. "Bible speaks agin it."

"Shaw. Shaw. We come a long ways. We got money to--"

"I do some tradin," the preacher blurted.

Dad opened the truck door. "Let's see what you got."

We walked among the dogs for about an hour. Dad and Reek looked at the teeth of some, feet and legs of others.

"That thar-un ain't mine," the preacher said, when they picked out one that looked like it would hunt. "Trainin him for a lawyer over in Asheville."

"I'd bet the fellow would sell him." Dad said.

The preacher pointed to a small female with a pointed nose and droopy eyes. "Registered Plott from up above Waynesville."

"Shaw. Shaw. You don't say!" Reek moved toward the small dog that had to be the sorriest excuse for a hunting dog I ever saw. It was either too lazy or too sick to stand.

I moved away to keep from listening to the preacher and spotted a white dog tied to some laurel bushes up in a hollow. He looked like a Dalmatian, but the black spots were smaller. More like pepper sprinkled on a sheet.

He wagged his tail like a pup when I started toward him. He jumped at the chain like he'd known me all his life. His face was so friendly he seemed to smile. I was so busy petting him; I didn't see Dad and them as they came up beside me.

"What you found?" Dad held out his hand for the dog to lick. "He's a big ol' pup." .

"He's well bred," the preacher said.

"Part fiest." Dad said, while he rubbed the dog's head. "Look at them little ears."

"Shaw. Shaw. For a fact," Reek added. "Hit don't look like no huntin dog to me."

"Preacher, what do you want for the big ugly pup?" Dad said.

I couldn't believe my ears.

"Bible speaks against puttin the price on a dog's head," the preacher said again. He squirmed in his tracks. I could see he wanted to sell the dog, and he almost set a price. He looked back at all the dark colored hounds, with big floppy ears, tied around the hillside.

"Just want the big pup for the boy," Dad said.

"Shaw. Shaw," Reek said. "We're a'wastin good time. Give you ten dollars."

The preacher pranced around a bit. For a minute, I thought he might be fixing to take off running down the mountain. Then he stopped and rubbed his beard with his dirty hand. I thought he was gonna have some kind of a fit.

"A good coon dog will fetch neigh on to a hundred dollars." The preacher ran his fingers through his beard like he was pondering, praying, or something or other.

"This'n here don't peer to be a good-un." Reek reached down and lifted one of the dog's ears. "Hit's ears ain't as big as a Bull Durham tobacky pouch."

The preacher took the ten-dollar bill from Dad and put it in his breast pocket. I led the big speckled dog down toward the truck. Everything I thought I knew about dog trading had been turned upside-down.

"All big ears are good for," I said, "is to get all bloody when a dog chases somethin through a briar thicket."

"We are some dog traders." Dad grinned and reached under the seat and brought out a fruit jar of white liquor. "We went off and bought us this firehouse dog."

"Shaw. Shaw." Reek took a drink from the jar without taking out his snuff. "I've seen bigger ears on half-grown squirrels."

I looked back at the dog laying against the back glass. He looked like a white dog all covered with black specks of soot. "I'm gonna call him Speck," I said.

"For sure, we won't name him after that lyin preacher." Dad said. "We didn't even get his name."

The smell of liquor, snuff, and Reek's old coat filled the truck cab. Dad and Reek were having a great time telling hunting and fishing tales. I went to sleep with my head on Reek's shoulder.

We turned up into Rail Cove just before dusky dark. Dad and Reek had drunk the whole jar. The truck hadn't got stopped good when our dogs caught sight of Speck. They came tearing up from every direction. They barked and growled so loud, I couldn't hear myself think. The hounds got their courage up, spoiling for a fight. They jumped as high as they could, biting hunks out of the truck bed. Fangs showed--bristles turned straight up.

"They'll kill my dog!" I said.

Dad and Reek were in no shape to do little of anything about it. All at once, Speck jumped off the truck and landed on the big hound Dad had hit with the tobacco stick. This time the fight was serious. Fur flew in every direction. Blood gushed from gashes cut by Speck's long teeth. He slung one dog up against the truck wheel so hard the whole truck rocked.

Dad came to life when he saw what was taking place. "He's gonna kill all my huntin dogs!"

"Shaw. Shaw. Shaw," was all Reek could say; yet, snuff flew every which-a-way.

It was over in less than a minute. All the hounds were at least twenty yards away from the truck. Most of them just whimpered and licked their wounds. Only a couple uttered low growls-- from forty feet away.

"Shaw. Shaw. He licked that whole pack of dogs--without raisin a bristle."

Dad held on to the truck with both hands. "He let them know right fast who's boss of the lot."

"Shaw. He's got the speed to go with them fiest ears."

Speck came up to me wagging his tail and licked my hand as if nothing had happened. I rubbed him from head to tail. He didn't have a cut anywhere that I could find.

Sometime during the night, I woke up scared. What if the dog had left? They do sometimes. There was something I'd forgot. I had to do it right then. I hurried to Mama's sewing box to get a pair of scissors.

"What in the world are you doing?" Dad struck a match.

"Speck may have left. They try to make their way to where they came from."

"Cain't it wait til morning?" Mama said.

"No way." I found the scissors and fumbled toward the front door. I headed for the woodshed.

Outside, the moon was nearly full, and I saw Speck laying on the porch under the window by where I sleep. He wagged his tail, which caused it to make a thumping sound against the wall. I motioned for him to come so the noise wouldn't wake up everybody in the house. I petted him for a few minutes, then took the scissors and cut some of the hair from the tip of his tail. He followed me when I went to bury it under the doorstep.

I laid down with my back against the wall and pulled Speck up in front of me. Now his tail couldn't hit the wall. With the hair under the doorstep, he wouldn't ever leave. I woke up as daylight first broke over Weatherman Bald.

The next night we went hunting over in the Nantahala River section; as always we took every dog we owned. It was warm and damp.

"Shaw," Reek said, "coons'll be a'travelin.'"

"You seem fidgety," Dad said to me.

"I just hope Speck will at least follow the pack," I said.

"He don't look much like a hunter." Dad's face got grim. "If he won't hunt we'll have to leave him at home."

We parked a little after dark on the rim that overlooked the gorge. I lit my pine-knot torch to give Reek enough light to get his old railroad lantern going. Dad had a big five-cell flashlight, but we only used it to spot a coon in a tree.

"Hyar! Hyar!" Dad called the dogs to him. He didn't want them to smell the coal oil Reek always spilled when he tried to fill the lantern.

"I hope my dog don't fall off one of them cliffs," I said to Reek.

"Shaw. Shaw. Dogs are born to run things. They wouldn't have it no other way."

We followed the narrow trail past the cliffs. The sound of the roaring river below made it scary, but my torch cast a good light, it being fresh and all. Besides, it wasn't these cliffs where the dog got killed. Anyway, they were safe as long as they weren't running on a hot track.

An hour later we came to some flat woods. My torch was dim as a match. A saw-briar wrapped around my head and dang near tore my left ear off. The blood running down my neck felt like a lot. When I put my hand on it, it had done and clotted. I was still rubbing my ear when I caught up with Dad and the dogs in a low gap leading to a fair-sized hollow.

The dogs stayed under our feet--to catch their breath like I did. Speck was out a ways by himself; he held his head high in the air.

"I believe Speck has winded something," Dad said.

"Shaw. Yes." Reek stood still as a fence post, the way he always did when he listened or watched.

"Must be a bear or wildcat," Dad whispered. "Got to be a real strong scent."

Speck leapt out of sight. The other dogs took off after him. It was quiet as they tried to straighten out the trail. Dad and Reek stood so still a body couldn't tell they were breathing. Only the flicker of the lantern broke the still of the dark, damp night.

"That Speck dog's barkin treed," Dad said, soon as he heard the first barks from way down in the hollow.

Nobody moved a muscle. "Shaw. Shaw. I believe your right. I know all the others' voices."
Dad took off in a lope; Reek and I followed as best we could.

"Shaw," Reek muttered. "How he can see in this pitch dark without a light is a puzzlement."

When we reached Dad, Speck was at the foot of a big beech tree. He jumped and barked with every breath--never took his eyes off the top limbs. Soon, the other dogs caught up and joined in.

"What do you think, Reek?" Dad asked.

"Shaw. Let's believe in him til he gives us cause to doubt."

We spread out to get a better look. I went to the upper side of the tree.

"I see him," Dad said. "Looks like a big boar coon to me. Up there on the second limb from the top!"

Dad pulled his long-barreled pistol out of his coat and held it with his right hand. With his left, he held the flashlight against it. Then the coon was easy to see. Its eyes shined like two green candles.

Dad fired. The blast sounded like thunder in the damp air. The flash lit up the dark hollow like it was day.

It was a long ways to the coon. He just sat still; I figured the shot had missed. Then he tumbled out of the tree and landed in the gully off to the right.

The dogs were on him at once. Almost as fast as the dogs, Reek had the coon by his hind legs. He got all the dogs to turn loose except Ol' Lead. Dad had to blow in the dog's ear before it would give up and let go.

"Shaw. Shaw. He's a dandy coon!" Reek held the coon over his head. "Biggest dad-blamed coon we've caught in a spell!"

"Maybe ever," Dad said.

Then Speck commenced to bark not thirty yards away. He howled like he had before.

"Shaw. False trail, I'll bet. It's where this old coon traveled a while back."

"Best give the big dog his dues," Dad said as he headed out. "He ain't lied yet."

It took a little longer to find the second coon. He moved three or four times, always keeping his eyes turned away from the light. Then I saw him. He looked big as a cub bear. Dad saw him too. In a few minutes, we had both the coons laying by a hemlock tree. I knew the hunt was over for that night. Dad loved to hunt, but he didn't believe in killing more than we would eat.

"Earned your keep tonight, big boy." Dad patted Speck on the head.

"I guess we'll take him along next time," I said.

"Reckon we better field-dress these." Dad handed one of the coons to Reek. "It'll still be a load to tote out."

Reek rolled the coon over on its back. "Shaw, yes. Hit's a long pull back to the truck."

"Best we done in a single night in years," Dad said as he tied the two coons together and slung them across his back.

Two nights later we went on a hunt over on Dirty John Creek. The air was much colder, and a high wind howled overhead. It never got down as low as the treetops, but it roared like thunder.

An hour after we got there, the dogs struck a cold track. They trailed it for three hours, all the way over to Muddy Bottoms and back. We built up a fire and waited.

"Shaw. Shaw," Reek said, "I ain't heard Speck open one time on that track."

"I saw somethin white movin up on that far ridge," I said. "Must be Speck."

Dad stomped around on the froze ground. "I reckon it was."

The sharp smell of burning leaves made my nose run, so I walked down to the branch. Again, I saw the white shape of something way up on the hillside.

An hour later, things heated up. The dogs had jumped something. They made a beeline for Bear Wallow Creek. We sat and listened as they crossed the low ridges to the east.

"Got to be a deer or a ridge-runnin fox," Dad said.

"Shaw, there ain't no use tryin to call them off."

"Their feet will be so sore we cain't hunt them for a week."

Speck barked like he had something treed up on the mountainside. This lasted a good fifteen minutes, and then he stopped as sudden as he had started. Dad and Reek stood still and listened. Five minutes later, Speck barked again.

Things went on like that several times over the next hour. Speck lit in and barked like he had a coon up pert-near every tree on the mountain. Then he hushed.

"If I didn't know better, I'd swear he was tryin to call the other dogs off," Dad said. "He's barkin treed all over that mountain."

"Shaw, I'll bet you're right." Reek warmed his hands over the fire. "I've heard of dogs that smart in my time, but I never seed one."

Dad nodded at me. "Go see what he's up to."

I went up the mountain in the direction of the barking. Twice Speck moved as I got closer. Had he got two coons treed at once? In my heart, I knew better. Still, something just wasn't right. I whistled. The barking stopped. Then started again, farther up the mountain. Twenty minutes later I reached the spot. I searched and searched. No barking. No dog.

A little later, I got a glimpse of him crossing the hollow just above me. I whistled again. Speck turned and came down to me like he'd just found out that I was hunting for him. He had a sheepish look on his face.

Once I got back to the fire, I told them what had happened.

"Shaw," was the only thing either said.

It had been two hours since we'd heard the others. Dad took off his hunting coat and laid it over behind a log near where we parked the truck. Dawn was just cracking when we left for home, with one dog and no meat.

The next two days we returned to Dirty John, but had no luck. Every night we planned where we would look the next day. Dad would take his single-barreled shotgun. He'd break it down and blow through the barrel; it made a low moaning sound that carried for miles. On the fourth day, we found two of the young dogs on Dad's coat.

With us gone dog hunting every bit of free time we had, and most of the dogs still in the woods, things were quiet around the house. My youngest sister played with Speck; she thought he was a pony.

"Shaw. Shaw," Reek said every evening when we started home. "We ain't got enough dogs to go rabbit huntin."

After two more weeks, we got word through the mailman that a woman over on Moccasin Creek had our dogs. We headed out early the next morning as a light snow began to fall. Moccasin was a long creek that runs halfway across the county; it was about seventy miles over there by the road.

We came upon an old woman skidding pine poles down the dirt road. Dad asked where the woman lived that was keeping our dogs.

"She lives way back, betwixt here and Moccasin Top," said the old woman.

Early in the evening, we found the house. The snow had turned to little blue ice balls that sparkled in the winter sun. A woman with a big apron and men's boots was up behind the house, picking persimmons from a low bush, thrashing them off with a cane pole.

"Got to pick these while the weather's cold. Best to do it when frost is still on the things." She talked as if she'd known us for a long time. "But I suspect they'll never know once they're in the jar."

"What are you goin to use them for?" Dad said.

"Plan to make me some persimmon beer."

"Are you the woman who has the stray dogs?" Dad said.

"Come here four days ago. Skin and bones they aire."

"Shaw. They been gone a time and a time," Reek allowed.

"Peers they been livin on skunks," She said. "They smell to the high heavens."

I was sure glad Speck didn't smell like no skunk, with him sleeping on the porch under my window. Mama wouldn't put up with any skunk odor near the house.

"I do truly thank you for puttin them up," Dad said. "I can pay you."

"No you cain't. My man Ike Fowler kept dogs all his days."

"I knew Ike," Dad said, "Met him when I was just a boy."

Reek took his hat off his bald head. "Shaw. Shaw. He was the best hunter in these Mountains for many a day."

I climbed the persimmon tree and gathered the fruit for her while Dad and Reek brought the dogs down from the barn.

"Be two weeks before they're ready to hunt." Dad lifted Ol' Bell up onto the truck.

"Shaw. Shaw. A little belly timber works wonders."

"Bet Mama will make us keep them in the barn til the skunk scent goes away," I said.

A week later we started hunting again.

One year while hunting season was in full swing several of our dogs came up missing. Sometimes the dogs would go hunting on their own, maybe even for a day or two, but never this time of year. Not when we hunted them almost every night.

"Shaw. Shaw," Reek said, a few nights later. "Speck, Bell, and Ol' Blue, them thar was the best dogs in these here parts."

Dad and Reek talked about the missing dogs every night. Dad asked everybody he met down in the settlement.

We headed for the feed store at the crack of dawn Saturday morning. We sat in the old truck a good hour before the feed store man came. As he flung open the big double doors, mice ran everywhere.

"Confound that worthless cat!" He swatted at a big yellow cat perched on a bale of hay.

"That ol' tomcat's so fat he's about to pop," Dad said. "There's enough mice in here to feed a train load of alley cats."

"I reckon," the feed store man said as he poured a big bowl of milk out for the cat.

Dad asked if he had heard anything about the dogs.

"No, but I'll ask about."

We left for town. Dad asked everybody down at the poolroom about the dogs.

Some of our neighbors that lived at the mouth of the cove said they saw a strange car with a

Georgia tag a few days ago. "It come down out of the cove just hittin the high spots," Mrs. Wordlaw said. "I do believe it was full of dogs."

We never got any other word. I missed having Speck around. At nights, I laid awake and listened for him to bark. Mama said, "You mope around like you had lost your last friend."

I missed the hunting. We did go hunting a few times while the weather was warm, but it seemed to have lost most of its charm.

Just before Christmas, Dad got a one-line letter: "That Preacher who stolt yourn dogs moved to Georgy."

Dad carried the letter in his bib pocket and read it several times a day.

"I figure it was wrote by a woman," Dad said.

Reek spit snuff into the fireplace. "Shaw. And I figure she was talkin about the preacher that went and sold us Speck."

"Come this weekend we're going to hunt them dogs," Dad said.

Reek came down with the shingles that week and was laid up in the bed. Saturday morning Dad and I left home well before daybreak.

There were no dogs tied in the woods where the preacher had lived. I stood in the yard when Dad went up on the porch. A man I'd never seen came to the door. Dad must have known him, though, because he called him by name when he showed him the letter.

The man shook his head no, but I could see a woman nod her head "yes," through the window curtains beside the chimney.

"Do you know where the preacher moved?" Dad asked.

"Down Georgia way. Place called Ironduff."

The man leaned his cane up against his belly and took an envelope from the breast pocket of his overalls. His hand trembled as he handed it to Dad.

Dad looked at it for a minute then handed the envelope back. "Thanks."

Back in the truck, I asked, "Did they know where the preacher went?"

"For a fact," Dad said. "They sent the letter."

"I heard him say he didn't."

"He didn't lie. His woman sent the letter. Don't forget, he didn't tell me the address; he only handed me the envelope."

"I see," I said, "I think."

At the forks of the Nantahala River, we didn't turn toward home. We followed the winter sun southwest; neither of us talked much.

I laid my head down and felt the pistol under the quilt we used to cover the ragged truck seat. Dad seemed to know where we were going--we didn't have to ask directions one time. He also seemed to be dead-set to get there in a hurry.

Maybe four hours later, we were riding down this red clay road when we came up on a bright red sign on a fence post: COON DOGS FOR SALE

"Why does he sell dogs here, when he wouldn't price them back home?"

Dad gave no answer. He hit the brakes and turned off down the muddy road. It was a long ways before we came to a house.

"How do you know this is where he lives?" I said.

"I just do."

A few minutes later we came to a frame house, a much nicer house than what the preacher had lived in before. It even had paint on it. There was a sign like the one on the fence, only this one was nailed to a porch post.

Dad didn't slow down when we got to the yard. He drove the truck right up to the porch steps. He reached under the quilt, picked up the pistol, and stuck it into his hunting coat pocket.

"Is your man home?" he asked the heavyset woman that came to the door.

"He's asleep. Hunted last night, he did."

"Wake him up--I want to talk to him now!"

Just then, the preacher came to the door, dressed in dirty hunting clothes. I could see Dad's jawbone twitch as he stared the preacher in the eye, only inches away. "I come for my dogs. I don't want any trouble, but I'm ready if that's what it takes."

The preacher backed up a step. "I'm a preacher--I cain't tell a lie. I took the dogs--I truly missed the one you bought off me somethin awful."

"Where are they?" Dad said.

"Just a minute . . . we can make a lot of money, you know. These people down here will buy anything that resembles a coon dog. These swamp coons are easy to catch. Don't take much of a dog. You could buy them up in the mountains, and could--"

"I'm going to say this just one more time," Dad said. "I've come for my dogs."

"I've got the white dog and the female," the preacher said, "but I sold the blue dog."

I thought for sure that Dad was going to hit him in the mouth. Dad's face got redder and redder--his fists clenched. He stepped closer and stared in the preacher's face for what seemed like forever.

"I'll pay you for the dog now." The preacher reached for his wallet. "Whatever you want."

"No you won't. Where is the dog now?"

"I sold him to a doctor in town," the preacher answered. "Got a good price for him."

"Well, I'll tell you what's about to happen. We're a going into town now. We'll be back by the crossroads later tonight, and you'll have all my dogs there. Ever last one."

"What time will you be back?" the preacher said.

Dad stuck his finger right up in the man's face. "Whatever time it is, you be there."

It was way past dark when we got done eating and filling the truck with gas. It seemed to me that we were taking more time than we needed--we even ate at a cafe with tables. The one back home only had a counter. It was made out of marble, and while you ate, you had to keep killing the ants that came up through the cracks.

I fretted at what Dad would do if the preacher didn't do what Dad had told him. The preacher seemed to count on his tongue to get him out of trouble. If the preacher wasn't at the crossroads, Dad would go back to the house, and his mind would be on hunting, except, the preacher would be the one hunted.

We got to the crossroads way in the night. I felt better when I saw the preacher standing by the fence. With ever last one of our dogs tied to it.

Not a word passed between us, but on the way home I realized for the first time how lucky I was to have him for a dad. He was as good a judge of men as he was of dogs.

I had heard people in town say you could tell how much a man was worth by how many dogs he had--the more dogs he had, the poorer he was.

Well, I felt mighty proud and rich that night as we crossed the state line, with a truckload of dogs.

"Lets go groundhog huntin tomorrow," Dad said, one early fall night.

"Shaw, I sure could use a mess of groundhog, biscuits, and apple sauce," Reek said. "Like your woman cooks."

"Give us a chance to toughen up the dogs," I said.

We had no more than got the truck stopped when the dogs hit a hot track. They baled off the truck and the race was on.

"It's a bear." Dad pointed to the soft ground. "Here's its bed, still warm."

"Shaw. Shaw. Look at this track. It's big as a frying pan."

"Them dogs don't know how to tree a bear!" Dad said. "That big bear will kill them dogs if they bay him. Dog gotta know how to worry him, nip him on the heel and run."

"Shaw, shaw."

Dad broke to run after the dogs. "Hyar! Hyar!"

We ran straight west, toward a low gap a half a mile away. My lungs almost busted but we kept on running. We heard the fight before we got there. It sounded like the end of time. Barks, growls, and whines filled the air.

The grunts the bear made caused my hair to stand on end. It sounded like a bull that had been caught in a noose. Only much louder.

"Hyar! Hyar!" Dad yelled.

When we got to the gap, I saw a huge laurel thicket ahead. It seemed to go on forever. A hundred feet below us, the laurel broke as the bear threw the dogs around like pillows. Every time another dog leapt on him, the bear slapped it away, tearing big gashes in the dog's hide.

Dad jerked the pistol out of his coat and took off into the thicket ahead. I followed as fast as I could, sometimes on my knees. When we reached the spot, dogs laid dead and dying all over the ground. All the laurel bushes in a twenty-foot strip had been knocked down like a big boulder had rolled over them.

Dad jerked off his coat and tended the hurt dogs. Reek ran up and did the same. The smell of fresh blood was sickening.

I looked for Speck. He was nowhere to be found. In a few minutes, we had three of the least hurt dogs bandaged up. I heard Dad shoot. A few seconds later he shot again, then again, and again.

"Got to put these others out of their misery," he said. Tears and sweat ran down his face.

"Shaw. What a waste. What a waste," Reek said.

"Listen!" I said. "I hear Speck trailin off toward the river. At least he's still able to run. We need to follow him."

"No need," Dad said. "We cain't cross the river where they're headed."

"Shaw, we wouldn't be able to crawl through this thicket in three days."

When we got done tending and burying the dogs in the stump hole, Dad pointed to the log. "It looks like the dogs leaped off an old hemlock log onto the bear. He cleared the thicket with them."

Back in the truck, we drove all the way around the thicket twice. We stopped on every knoll and listened. We never heard a sound out of Speck.

I could tell by Dad and Reek's faces they wanted to get the bear as bad as I did. He was somewhere in the laurel thicket. Only where? It was at least ten miles square.

Dad and Mama sewed the other three dogs up where the bear had ripped their sides with his giant claws. Two of them died the next night.

I found Speck on Dad's coat a week later at the place the chase had started. He looked gaunt but considering the wear and tear, he was in fine shape. He had tore his collar almost in half on the laurel bushed. I bought him a new one the next Saturday. He slept for two whole days and was back to his old self. He even let my younger sister use him for a pony, to pull a doll carriage.

Dad didn't get right back into coon hunting. It takes a long time to get the right mix of dogs he claimed. Dad and Reek didn't care much for hunting without dogs. They called it still-hunting. Mainly it was me taking Reek, after I got to driving.

After I got to taking the truck out courting at night, Speck started doing a peculiar thing.

Late in the night, he would hear me come up the cove in the old truck, and bark treed up on the ridge behind the house. It happened more times than I could count.

"Go see what your dog has treed," Mama said.

"He don't have nothin treed. He just wants to trick me off up there so I'll go hunting with him."

"Go see, anyway. If he does have somethin treed he'll bark for three solid days and nights."

When I got to where he'd been barking, he was another fifty yards higher up, barking again. Once I reached the top of the ridge, he would come to me. He'd wag his tail like crazy and make low sounds in his throat as if to tell me he wanted to go hunting. It was kind of a game we played.

Late one summer, Speck got so feeble he wouldn't hold his head up, unless I spoke to him or patted his head.

The evening he died, I buried him down by the barn. Even carved a wooden marker, which got plowed under the next spring.

There was no sign of Speck ever daddying any pups. To my knowledge there were never any gray-colored pups born in Rail Cove.

Sometimes, on a clear fall night, I take his cracked leather collar down from the porch sill. If I stand perfectly still, I can hear him bark way up on the mountain.

TWIDGE -- It'll Beat a Snowball

"A letter came today," Mama said, "Bell is sending her boy Louin here to go huntin with you."

"The hell you say!" Dad said. "We ain't heard hide nor hair of her in five years." Dad got up from the table. "Got to go clean some bee gums."

He did that a lot when something didn't suit him. Talking about Bell never did.

"That baby sister of yourn was powerful headstrong, "Aunt Nica said to him as he went out the door, "even while she wus a young'un."

"She's your sister too," Mama said to Aunt Nica. "Don't forge--"

"Where does Aunt Bell live, anyway?" I said.

"She went to Charlotte to work when she was barely grown," Mama said. "Never came back."

A lot of people go off to them cotton mill towns. I'd even heard Dad say he might have to, if times got really hard.

"Where is Charlotte?" My younger sister said.

"It's a far piece off," Mama said. "Your Dad reasoned that Bell ought to come home as soon as she had enough money to get on her feet like other folks."

"Well, how old is this boy Louin?" I said.

"He ain't no boy," Mama said, "he's a right smart older than you--I believe he's twenty past."

"When does he get here?" I said.

"He's coming on the bus when it runs day after tomorrow."

I went outside when I saw Reek Moore coming down the cove. He looked like a fodder stack, with both arms full of tarpaulin; he even had some wrapped around his neck. His hands were full of every old piece of camping gear you could name.

He flung the whole mess up on the back of Dad's truck. "Shaw, we got us a bunch of tarp. C.C.C. boys gived it to me. No brush-harbor camp this time."

I didn't say nothing; the stuff was mostly just rags. But anything would beat a bunch of pine tops if it were to rain. Reek didn't waste time when it came to hunting and fishing, even though we weren't leaving yet for three days.

"Shaw, boy, you dig us lots of bait," Reek said. "We're apt to be gone a time and a time."

I dug a gallon lard bucket full of worms and got two wasp nests off the corncrib. I kept spring lizards in a barrel to sell. They brought a dime a dozen, from city folks when they came here to fish.

I don't reckon, they knew you could catch spring lizards up any branch. It took me a few minutes to catch more than enough for our trip. I caught out thirty red lizards and put them in another lard bucket. They're scarce so they are worth a nickel apiece. Anyway, we had plenty of both.

"Shaw, Shaw. Them's the biggest wasp nestes I ever seed," Reek said, when he saw me coming from the crib.

By the time I got to the truck, he had half the bed covered with stuff. "Shaw yes, we got enough rations to last a month and, for a fact, we'll git some game."

Reek went back up the cove for another load while I put fresh moss in the worm bucket. I followed Dad back into the house. I wanted to know more about this Louin.

"Bell was a very pretty girl," Mama said as I came up on the porch. "Made a good life for herself out there."

Dad molded the bee's wax with his hand and pondered for a spell. "Yeah, but she never came back even for family matters."

"Maybe now she's had a change of heart," Mama said.

I turned and went back out to the truck shed. I sure wasn't going to find out anything from them. All they wanted to talk about was Bell. Besides, Reek would be back soon.

"We're gonna have us a partner on this trip," I said, as soon as Reek drug a big wooden box up on the truck.

"Shaw, I declare."

"My Aunt Bell's boy, Louin. Dad don't seem none too fond of Aunt Bell."

"Shaw, hain't so. Last winter the Crofts come in from out near where she lives. Me and yore Dad tramped all the way to the head of High Lonesome Creek, in the rain, jist to inquire about her."

"I see." I climbed up on the truck bed to store things away, while I tried to get it all straight in my head.

"Shaw, they told us she married a tooth dentist, she did."

We were about finished when Dad walked up. "We'll camp up on Brushy Face."

"Shaw, a body can cover a heap of ground from thar."

I was just glad we were going to a place where we could drive into the camp, in place of toting all our stuff. On some of the trips, we'd carried everything for miles.

By nightfall, we had the truck loaded and I still didn't know a thing about this boy except that they called him Twidge.

When the time came, I went with Dad to the bus station. There were only two passengers on the bus, because it turned around here and went back to

Atlanta. One of the passengers had on an army uniform so it was easy to figure out which one was which.

Twidge was a big fellow by our standards; he was over six feet tall and two hundred pounds or better. He carried more around the middle than any of our folks did that I'd met. His hair was sandy colored with a cowlick on the left side. He didn't say much when we got out to the truck. I figured it was because he had his mouth full of candy.

He sat in the truck while Dad and I went into Miller's Mill for a few things. I got the feeling Twidge would rather be somewhere else.

"You ever laid out in the woods before?" Dad asked.

"What?" Twidge said.

"Did you ever go camping?" I said.

"I went to a boys camp in the summer," Twidge said.

Dad didn't say much else until we got home. Mama had supper cooked and we went to bed well before dark.

"Reek'll be here by four-thirty, talking about what a late start we're gettin," Dad said as he blew out the lamp.

"I've got a feeling about this weather," Mama said, the next morning.

Dad didn't answer. He just sipped his coffee and seemed to be pondering on it.

Breakfast was over by five o'clock. Reek had loaded the dogs on the truck before he came into the house. Twidge looked funny when Reek drunk coffee and dipped snuff at the same time.

"I didn't hear him knock before he came in," Twidge whispered to me.

I thought for just a second. "He don't never."

Reek grabbed his old felt hat and headed for the door. "Shaw, we're a'burnin up daylight."

"We'll be back by the time the tobacco is ready to work off," Dad said.

He got up and followed Reek out. I could tell that was not the way Twidge thought a camping trip ought to start.

It took the better part of the day to get to the mouth of Brushy Face Creek. We stopped to eat at a spring up on the side of Gun Barrel Ridge. I felt like Twidge was beginning to like it better; he kept on eating.

"Shaw, hit's warmed up considerable," Reek said.

"You boys ride on the back," Dad said. "Keep them dog boxes from sliding off on the rough road up ahead."

Twidge sat on a box and leaned back against the truck cab. I sat on Dad's side and watched the road ahead, not so much to see where we were going, but to keep Reek from spitting snuff all over me.

"That old man Reek sure has a funny way of speaking," Twidge said. "I've never been around anyone that backwards before."

I started to say that Reek was as much at home in the mountains as Twidge was in the city when a big oak limb hit Twidge across the shoulder blades. It lifted him off the dog box and knocked him back toward the rear of the truck. Only the big stack of tarpaulin kept him from going over the end gate.

Twidge looked at the truck cab as if he expected Dad to stop. I knew Dad wouldn't. Twidge was more careful then; after his first wetting, he even learned how to not get wet when we forded a river.

The fall weather had been dry enough for us to drive blame-near to the head of the creek. We parked under some big hemlock trees that stood between a spring and the creek.

"Shaw," Reek allowed, "that old chestnut sog looks pert-near as big as it did the last time I built a fire agin it, when I call back the time."

"Just growed itself a new cover of moss," Dad said. "It's been nigh on to twelve years, now that I think about it."

Twidge looked at me. "What are they talking about?"

"That old log is all soggy," I said. "Reek just calls it a sog to save time."

"This is sure not like my scoutmaster talked," Twidge said.

Dad and Reek cut poles and built a big lean-to in front of the log. Twidge seemed not to have any idea what was taking place, but he did help me get the dogs tied up without saying a word.

"If we'd made better time," Dad said, "I'd have us a mess of speckled trout for supper."

Reek threw a slab of pork onto a big flat rock like it was a table. "Shaw, reckon we'll make do with this sowbelly. Hit'll stick to your ribs."

"This is not what I expected--I thought we'd have tents and running water," Twidge said as he watched me clean potatoes and onions down at the creek.

I didn't answer, but I knew if he didn't take a hold and pull some weight around here, Dad would dress him down in no easy terms.

Reek had made coffee and fried meat by the time we got back. He did most of the cooking. Being a bachelor man, he was used to it. Reek thought he was a good hand at cooking--he talked to the food all the time: "Lay flat thar little tater, so's I can brown you good'n bro . . ."

Dad had slipped off up the creek and came back with four fair-sized trout all cleaned and ready. Reek laid them in a big tin skillet.

"Reek," Dad said," you stir that food all the time, you'll wear it out."

"Shaw." Reek never stopped stirring. "It ain't kilt you yet; apart from that hit'll beat a snowball." He flipped the bones out with a fork until all that was left in the pan was pieces of fish. The smell of cooking hung low in the hemlocks, causing my belly to growl. I wished Reek would quit piddling with the food and let us eat.

"Look! He's getting snuff into the food!" Twidge said.

"Spits snuff into everything he cooks," I said.

Twidge's face wrinkled up, but he ate heavy anyway. He took out a rag and blotted his lips after every bite. That tickled me.

After we had finished eating and fed the dogs, Dad said, "You boys clean this mess up."

"Where's the soap and hot water?" Twidge said.

Dad looked at him like he hadn't heard a word. Reek almost blew out the lip full of snuff he had put in just a minute before.

"We'll get some from the spring," I said.

"I'm not sure spring water is safe," Twidge said. "Back in Charlotte we have city water. Do you suppose there is a well nearby?"

"Shaw," Reek said, "when the Maker gets water fit for drinking he sends it to the top of the ground."

With all the cooking things I could carry, I headed to the spring." I'll show you how we clean them with branch water," I said

When I rubbed the pots with a handful of mud and sand, I could see Twidge's eyes open wide. I threw the sand into the bushes and polished the inside with white sand. Twidge's mouth flew open as I held the pan up to see if I'd missed any spots.

By the time we finished, Dad and Reek had cut and stacked almost a cord of birch wood up near the fire. Sparks rose into the trees. It was a good thing, for the late fall gnats swarmed just outside the fire and smoke. Twidge slapped at them with both hands.

"You gonna play cards, or not?" Dad said to Reek.

"Shaw yes, I'll take your money." Reek raked the pine needles away with his hand and spread out his hunting coat. They lay down on the ground and started dealing.

Mama didn't hold to card playing at the house, so Dad and Reek played most every night that we were in the woods. They played a game called five-up, using small sticks to keep score. I never understood how, with the ground covered with sticks. I guess each one knew the other would never cheat.

"Put another log on my heap," Dad said to Reek. Dad had won the first hand.

"Shaw." Reek started dealing. "I'm a'fixin to show you where Noah hit the wedge. Next hand."

I went out by the fire and sat down by Twidge. I wanted to know more about the city. He told me about a picture show they built outside. A body watched from their car. I wouldn't care for that much; our old truck seat was just a pile of quilts anyhow, and the picture show house had good seats.

Twidge pulled out a thing called a sleeping bag, got into it, and closed the flap. It even had a pillow. I crawled over in the pile of tarps Reek had brought, pulled off my boots and used one for a pillow. Dad had already found him a rock for a pillow. He had laid it by the fire to get it warm.

I woke up an hour later. Reek was slapping his thigh with his hat and running through the fire. He must have been winning.

Bam! Bam, bam. Reek was cooking breakfast. I'd heard Dad leave the camp about an hour earlier.

"What time is it?" Twidge said.

"Shaw," Reek said, "we don't carry a timepiece, but I hear a squirrel barking way up yonder."

Twidge looked at all the stars. He crawled out of the sleeping bag shivering all over. Reek made room for him by the fire. It looked funny; a big young man hugging the fire, shaking like a leaf, while Reek stood back a ways like it was mid-July.

Twidge poured a cup of coffee from the boiling pot, like he saw Reek do.

"Be careful," I said, too late. Twidge had already burned his mouth. Nobody could drink coffee as hot as Reek did.

"Shaw, you boys ought to hunt the north side of Thunder-Struck Ridge. As I recollect, thar's a stand of hickory and two big walnut trees on that face. On up a ways at the old Stillman Place you'll find some Potts apple trees and a big June apple."

"If it's been twelve years since you've been here," Twidge said," you don't expect us to believe that."

"If'n it's like I tell you," Reek said, "you might be able to bring us some camp meat."

I hurried to get Twidge away. I was afraid he'd take out his madness, at being here, on Reek. Then, I was afraid Reek would use his big knife.

We never knew where Reek carried that knife. He would have the thing out and be using it faster than a cat can blink its eyes. The blade was over a foot long and it cut meat like a hot knife does butter. We all called it 'the sticker.'

Twidge and I walked for an hour, grading our way across three ridges and through two deep hollows. I could hear Twidge grumble--his breath coming in short gasps. "I'll bet that old man never went to school a day. He uses words I've never heard. He's too old to know how to set up a proper camp. They weren't a bit interested when I told them about the drive-in movie."

I was getting mighty sick of hearing it, so I walked faster and faster. Twice I got plumb out of his sight. I knew for a fact that Reek had never been to any kind of movie. Dad had only gone when Mama convinced him it had a good story.

"Foolishness--made up stuff," he would say.

"Are you sure we're not lost?" Twidge puffed like a train engine while he tried to keep up with me. "There must be an easier way than this to travel."

"No, we're not lost. If we don't stay high, we'll end up in that deer-slick laurel thicket below."

"You're trying to fool me," Twidge said.

"Some people don't follow game trails; me, I always do. Critters know how to get through, around, and over the mountains better than me. You go any darn way you please. I'll meet you back at camp."

He followed a few steps behind until we reached the old orchard. I kneeled down and looked under the trees. Several deer grazed some fifty yards away. I pointed with my gun without raising it to my shoulder.

Twidge took a step and straightened up, raised his gun and fired. Two more deer joined the herd; the ridge was covered with whitetails then, but they were way too far off for us to get a decent shot. I wondered what had come over him as he ran toward the apple trees. Did he think he could catch them deer?

"Did you see those deer?" he said, when he got back "I might have hit one."

It took me a spell to think of anything to say. "Too far away, I'd reckon." I picked up my gun and headed up the creek.

It wasn't long before No Fat Creek turned into one waterfall after another. They reached from one side of the canyon to the other. In places, we could go around them by climbing the steep banks. Most of the time, we had to use our hands to pull ourselves up waist-high ledges, then take three or four steps and do it again.

I heard Twidge mutter as the cold water dripped from his pants; an hour later I only heard heavy breathing.

"There's some pretty woods ahead," I said, feeling a little sorry for him. The climbing and mumbling made his face red as a beet.

A short time later the gorge widened out into a flat three hundred yards wide; the laurel thicket gave way to long, tall hickory, oaks, buckeyes, beech, and poplar.

"Gol-ly," Twidge said. "I thought all the big trees grew down in the valleys."

"Most do," I said.

"How did you ever find this place? This isn't the place that old fool sent us to. Is it?"

"Reek knows the woods and everything in'em, don't forget."

Nothing was moving; I sat down by a big chestnut stump and watched two hickory trees off to my right. Twidge made his way toward the east.

I thought about Reek and Twidge--how they differ. Reek would never say anything bad about another person. Reek kind'a lived and let live. Twidge could learn a lot from him if he'd only stop to consider.

Boom! Boom! Boom! We had timed it about right. The woods were coming alive. I saw two squirrels heading up my trees. I shot one then I heard Twidge shoot again. I killed five as they came to the hickory trees, all the while listening to Twidge shoot off to my left.

I heard Twidge running toward me long before he came into sight. He was holding two gray squirrels, two boomers, and a ground squirrel over his head. "I've run out of ammunition!" he gasped.

He took half my shells and ran back through the woods. I shot out three more squirrels in the next hour.

Twidge talked a mile a minute as we started back. He climbed over the falls, paying no mind to the wetting. "I'm going to kill me two or three deer when we get to them apple trees," he said.

I didn't have the heart to tell him the deer most likely wouldn't be back there this soon. I followed along some fifty feet behind. This time he slipped quietly to the edge of the clearing.

We sat under the apple trees and watched for any movement. I could tell he was beginning to realize he had missed his chance earlier.

Out of the corner of my eye, I saw something move. I didn't move a muscle for another minute. A spike buck walked through the trees, ever so slow and quiet. I had been wrong. This far back deer are not as wild as they are where they're hunted a lot. The deer turned its back. I touched Twidge's arm. He raised his gun and aimed. His arm trembled. I waited for him to shoot. The buck sensed us and started prancing around. Twidge jacked another shell in the chamber, then another and another. I waited for him to shoot. The buck must have found us; it bolted for the back of the orchard.

"Did you see that?" Twidge said. "I missed him every time! This gun don't shoot straight."

"You never fired."

"I sure as hell did. This gun is no damn good."

I reached down in the leaves, picked up the unfired shells, and handed two to him. He looked at them as if he didn't know what they were. For the longest time, Twidge stood there. His mouth came open. "What happened?"

"You took the buck-eagers. You run all them shells through the gun without pulling the trigger." I swung my gun over my shoulder and walked away.

I tried to hide the boomers and ground squirrels from Dad and Reek, but Twidge was proud of them and watched me clean every one. They were so little, I thought I had them hid pretty well among the gray squirrels. Dad didn't hold to killing anything you didn't eat; besides, shells cost a lot.

Dad held up one of the little critters. "Who killed this prize?"

A long silence followed. I knew he was gonna tear into Twidge any minute. Maybe I should have warned Twidge, back in the woods.

"Shaw, hit'll beat a snowball, if'n the weather sets in," Reek said.

I was sure Dad would say something to me for letting it happen. Anyway, Dad didn't push it, which made me feel good.

On up in the evening Reek cooked all the boomers and ground squirrels and threw them to the dogs when Dad and Twidge weren't looking. Dad had to know it, but he never made mentioned of them again.

Later, while we were eating, I thought Twidge would get sick at his stomach. He stared with his mouth open as Dad cracked a squirrel head with his knife handle and dipped the brains out, eating every last bit.

"Reek found a passel of groundhogs had been using," Dad said, the next morning.

"Shaw, for a fact. By the size of them holes they'd weigh a good twenty pounds."

Twidge never went near the dogs after we'd tied them up. I could tell right off, Twidge's idea of a hunting dog didn't match what we had. None of ours looked alike; they wouldn't pass for the same breed.

"Hyar!" Dad called, scaring Twidge with the sudden yell.

An hour later we were down along Sandy Mush, hunting the low hills ringing the swampland. The dogs trailed something off to the left. It was hard to tell anything for the thick willow bushes that covered the ground.

One dog barked several times, a few seconds apart at first, then every breath. "Ol Lead's hit a hot'un," Dad said.

"Shaw yes, hit appears to me like we got us a sight race."

"Yeah, there goes Speck and Bell, they hit it too!" Dad said.

Wrinkles came over Twidge's brow, like he was having a hard time figuring out what was going on.

"Reek and Dad knows ever dog by its bar--"

Dad broke in before I finished. "They treed that land-loper down yonder in the flat."

Reek and Dad bolted through the willows and briar thicket. Twidge stood like he was froze; he seemed to study the ground ahead. He used the shovel, trying to part the bushes. I didn't know if he was afraid, or what.

"Dad will want the shovel and mattock, now!" I said, bumping into Twidge.

"Which way should I go?" he said.

"Study long, study wrong," I passed him and hurried toward the sound of the dogs. I could hear him mumble as he followed along. He was all out of breath and scratched up by the time we reached Dad and Reek. Twidge's right ear was bleeding all over his coat. He tried to show the blood to Dad and Reek, but they didn't pay the least mind to it

Dad and Reek held the dogs away from the hole. They would turn one loose, Lead first, then Speck, then June. Each dog would try to crawl into the hole--bark and dig--dirt flew everywhere.

"Shaw, hit ain't deep, way them dogs are carrying on."

"Swamp hogs never are," Dad said, while he cut a willow bush and stripped the limbs and leaves off. He ran the stick back into the hole, pulled it out and said, "Not three feet deep."

"Shaw, I'll tell a man."

"Hold them dogs." Dad handed Lead by the collar to Twidge.

I held the others while Lead drug Twidge all through the thicket. I laughed a little under my breath. It was hard holding a dog by the collar, but not that hard.

Reek's knife came from somewhere and he cut a bigger willow bush, this time he trimmed the limbs a few inches long. He studied the fork in the top before he cut it. When he finished the end looked like a bent pitchfork.

Twidge looked lost. I wanted to tell him that Dad was going to twist the stick so it would get tangled in the groundhog's thick fur, but he was having all he could do, holding the dog.

Dad stuck the stick into the hole and twisted it around and around. When it suited him, he started to pull. The dogs were hard to hold. They pulled at their collars until they choked.

"Got'em," Dad said, as the ground hog cleared the hole.

Lead broke loose from Twidge and dived. He was almost on top of Reek and the groundhog when, in one smooth stroke from somewhere, Reek brought out the big knife and stabbed it through the groundhog's heart. The knife glazed Lead and cut a place three inches long down his side. He yelped and snapped at Reek.

Dad got right up in Twidge's face. "Boy, you get my dog cut, and I'll tend to you."

Reek kept that from happening by holding the groundhog over his head, while the dog jumped and jumped. I figured right then and there, I'd better keep Twidge with me and away from Dad and Reek. Besides, the sight of blood made Twidge look peakid.

"Them groundhogs are easy to catch," Twidge said, that night.

"That'en was," I said.

"How do you cook that thing?" Twidge asked as he watched Reek peel the skin away from the white fat on the groundhog. The big knife moved as if it was part of Reek.

"Shaw, first you par-bile him and throw the water out. Then you bile him again."

"Sounds easy," Twidge said.

"Shaw, then you take a clean rag and wipe him down. Git a pot, throw in some taters, onions, spicewood, and yerbs--like I keep in this here jar."

"Then you throw away the groundhog and eat the rag." Dad had heard enough. He knew Reek was just a'foolin. Dad liked groundhog the way Mama baked it, but he didn't care much for all Reek's "biling." The way they were acting, I knew the card game would be something that night.

The next day Twidge and I went hunting. We were sitting on a ridge above a branch, talking, when we saw a squirrel down below that seemed to be gathering moss. I wondered what in blazes it was doing. Twidge reached for his gun, but I held his arm.

By now, the squirrel had a round ball of gray moss in his front paws. He headed for the branch. We followed along, just to see what he was up too. The squirrel laid down in a pond on his back and held the moss up with his paws. I thought he would drown. In a flash the critter come tearing out of the water and was gone before either of us could get a shot off.

"What do you make of that?" I said.

Twidge didn't answer. We climbed down the bank to the branch. We could see the little ball of moss floating on the water. I kicked it up on the bank.

"My god," Twidge said, "what's that all over it?"

"Fleas," I said.

"Wait'll I tell someone about this," he said.

"Your apt to see lots of things in the woods that's better not told. Even if you tell it for the truth, folks will think you're the biggest liar ever been."

"I guess your right."

"Reek can tell stories that'll make your hair stand on ends, if'en they'd quit playing cards ever blessed night," I said.

The next day, Twidge wanted to go groundhog hunting with Dad and Reek. The dogs treed way up on Squaly Mountain. We dug after a groundhog all day. We moved big rocks and little ones. The hole changed directions every few feet.

"Shaw, he's packing dirt behind him," Reek said. "We'll have to dig around the face of the ridge to try to hit the hole again."

By late that evening, the whole mountainside was potted with waist-deep holes. Judging by the way the dogs acted, we weren't any closer to him than when we started. We were all wringing wet;

we hadn't had anything to eat nor a drop of water all day.

"Look here," Dad said, "another hole, way around here." We all spread out and looked for other openings to the rocky ground. There were many. In fact, there were so many the dogs couldn't pick up the groundhog's scent--or wouldn't. They had to be tired too, having spent the day digging and being held.

It was late that night when we led the dogs back into the camp. We ate a cold supper and went to bed. Dad and Reek were too tired to play cards, even.

The next two days I took Twidge with me. We had a bunch of fish in the pond down below the spring. Our stock of game was going up every day. I hadn't learned anything about the city that would make me want to go there.

The next morning, I went to the spring for coffee water before daylight. I turned up the wick on the lantern and held it close above the pond we'd made below the spring. The water was muddy and there was not a fish anywhere.

"The fish are all gone," I said, back at the camp, "except for parts--heads and fins--scattered all over the ground."

"Something got the fish?" Twidge said from his sleeping bag.

"The hell you say," Dad scrambled around putting on his boots.

We hurried back to the pond. Dad and Reek studied the sign.

Twidge didn't like to look at the dead fish much.

"What do you make of it, Reek?" Dad said.

"Bobcats, bobcats," Reek said. "I'd say four or five grown-uns and three kittens. Awful peculiar, they'd come this close to the dogs."

Dad didn't like to be out-done. "All I know is, we'll all fish today."

Fish bit good; by late evening we had half as many as before. Even Twidge caught four nice trout and one big hornyhead, which I threw back, when nobody was looking.

We gathered up about a mile below camp and the four of us walked up the river together. Something made us hurry. We were all hungry, I reasoned.

"Hells, bells," Dad said as we came into sight of the camp.

"Shaw, shaw."

We ran the last fifty yards. The camp was wrecked. Even the stack of firewood was scattered all over the clearing. Bits of tarpaulins were laying all over the ground. I don't think there was anything that wasn't ruined. Twidge's sleeping bag was in four pieces.

"What did this?" Twidge said.

"Shaw, everthing scattered thither and yon."

Twidge stayed back a'ways. Dad turned the dogs loose so they could get water. They were all foamy and sweaty. I helped Reek save what we could, which wasn't much: four potatoes and a few beans Mama had strung on a thread.

"Shaw, hunt the grease; we got'a have some shortnin."

"Who wrecked the camp?" Twidge said.

Dad came over to where we stood. "There must have been fifty hogs here."

What had been a truckload of goods when we left, I could carry in my arms now. Twidge, he wandered around like he was lost again.

"Shaw, we'll eat parched fish til we can kill us a hog, and render out some lard."

"We had better go home in the morning," Twidge said to me.

"Don't count on it," I said, "Dad'll want to kill us one of them wild hogs as soon as he can."

Reek had fish cooking on sticks over the fire in no time flat. By sun down, we'd put back up a make-do shelter.

Dad tried to get the dogs to trail the hogs, but they were all tuckered out, some had raw places around their necks where they had lunged against their chains. He finally gave up. "A blind man could track them hogs in the dark, and them damn dogs won't."

"Shaw, we'll kill us a big fat'un come morning and have grease to spare. Meat too."

"We don't have enough food left to stink up a skillet, that's for sure," Dad said.

Dad and Reek were looking off toward the west. It had turned a right smart colder, but there wasn't a cloud in the sky.

Next morning it was even colder, and a big black cloud had rolled in. Reek was cooking more fish and the last of the potatoes.

"Shaw, them clouds are coming straight out of Wiley's Mudhole, yonder."

"This camp is not sufficient if it rains," Twidge said as he got up from the scraps of his sleeping bag.

"Don't worry," Dad said, "it won't rain."

I didn't know what they were talking about, but didn't like the sound of none of it. They were way too solemn.

"What's it all about?" I said.

Reek pointed to the ground beside the campfire. "Shaw, don't rightly know what to make of it; 'pears like them ants worked all night making mounds around their hole."

I looked at the ground. It seemed like it always did to me.

"Shaw, I heerd squirrels cutting on them tall hickory trees all night long. Listen; you can hear the leaves rattle in the trees."

"So?" I said.

"When critters work at night," Dad said, "it's a sure sign of bad weather. When leaves rattle on the trees it's bound to snow."

Reek turned to walk away. "Shaw, hit clouded up on a frost. Another bad sign."

"Too early in the fall," I said.

"These old mountains ain't got no calendar," Dad said. "I've seen it snow in July."

We saw it coming up the valley like a giant gray wave. Snowflakes as big as saucers floated down like feathers. They soon had the ground covered. They smothered the fire out in fifteen minutes. We worked hard and fast. Each time we got the tarp stretched good and tight, the weight of the snow would bring it down on us.

Dad cussed as he tried to get the fire going. The air was so damp and heavy the smoke barely rose head high. "Somebody must have throwed shotgun shells in the wood pile, the way this confounded wood pops and carries on."

Reek looked toward the sky. "Shaw, I figured on a waterspout, not a blizzard."

"Perhaps we should go home," Twidge said.

"Hell fire," Dad said, "I cain't see the truck, how'd I see the road?"

I could tell Twidge was getting hungry; most days he'd nibble all day long--by then there wasn't a thing left to eat.

Reek reached deep into the pocket of his hunting coat. He dumped a pocket full of acorns, chestnuts, hickory nuts, birch bark, leaves, and some yellow berries the size of bantam eggs in a pot. I had no idea what some of the other things were. In a little while he had it boiling.

"What's he cooking?" Twidge said.

"You'll see," Dad said. "God only knows what-in-all he puts in that stuff."

"Reek calls it pauper's gruel," I said.

"That concoction tastes good," Dad said, "but it'll gripe your belly."

"Shaw, hit'll beat a snowball."

"Yeah," Dad said, "I know for a fact, you've got an iron stomach."

"Shaw, if'en I had some bear grease; a body can drink bear grease without hit hurting him nary a bit."

"For some reason unbeknownst to the world," I said to Twidge, "Reek, he can take on the biggest bait of that stuff you ever saw, and it don't gripe his belly. Anybody else gets sick enough to die."

There wasn't a dry place to sit down anywhere, so we ate standing up. All the talk about eating Reek's gruel hadn't done much good. Twidge ate as much as Reek--he was sick with the stomach gripes in less than an hour. He groaned, moaned, and yammered like a dying calf. I felt sorry for him.

"I took on a big bait two years ago and my belly hurt something fierce," I said to Twidge. "The only thing good about the stomach ache from the gruel is that it don't last but a couple of hours."

We made it through the night by keeping the snow beat off the roof. The snow was falling as hard at daylight as when it started.

"It looks like we'll have to tramp out," Dad said.

"Cain't we take the truck?" Twidge said, "it's a long way."

"Shaw, snow's up to the hood. That old truck, hain't no bull-snozer."

"Won't they come for us?" Twidge wanted to know.

"Not til spring," Dad said. "Our bones'll be bleached out white by then."

"Shaw, hit's a little walk, that's all."

"Carry some pieces of tarp," Dad said. "Might come in handy."

"Aren't we going to follow the road?" Twidge said as we started down the creek.

"Shaw, better to follow the creek, less snow down under the hem-pines."

"I'm afraid we'll get lost," Twidge said.

Dad and Reek laughed. I didn't say nothing. I rounded up a handful of pieces of tarp and hung them over my shoulders.

The going was hard; snow was up over my waist. The dogs were having as hard a time trailing

111

along behind. The first hour we hadn't covered much ground. The silence of the falling snow gave me a headache. There wasn't a sound we didn't make.

Dad came up with a way we could make better time. "We'll walk in single file. The lead man plows out sort of a path the rest of us can follow. When he gets plumb tuckered out he moves to the rear where it's the easiest."

Dad and Reek could stay up there for about an hour. Twidge and me gave out in far less time.

"How long will it take?" Twidge asked, for the forth time in the past hour.

"I guess we'll have to eat a couple of them dogs," Dad said, "before we get there."

Twidge never spoke the rest of the day. The snow went right on coming down--night fell and we plodded on.

My mind quit wondering about where we were and how long we could go on. I thought about how it must be to live in the city. I knew more than I let on from reading schoolbooks and papers. I'd heard of houses heated day and night by coal or oil delivered right to the door and ice boxes filled by a delivery man. Some even had electric refrigerators.

Mama and Dad seen to it that we had about everything a body could want for. It was plain, by the way Dad carried on, that he didn't care for city living. "Living out of a store" were the words he used when talk got around to living without a cow, garden, hogs, and such. I reckon he was right if an outside picture show is a thing them folks put a lot of stock in. I guess we ain't so bad off after all.

"Perhaps we can find a cave." Twidge jarred my mind back to where we were.

"We've passed some caves back a ways," Dad said, "but we cain't hold up in one, we'd freeze to death, wet as we are."

The snow gave off enough light when dark came that we could keep going. We hadn't been able to see twenty feet in front of us all day and the deafening silence went on and on.

Our faces got so cold we wrapped the pieces of tarp around our heads and plowed on. At times I felt like I was going to sleep, and Dad would put me up front every time I nodded off. That sure woke a body up.

"We must be lost," Twidge said, "we haven't forded a river or creek yet."

I thought about it, for a long time. He was right. Every time we came close to one you could hear it roaring a half a mile off, which to me was better than all the quiet of the falling snow.

"Why haven't we crossed the river?" I said to Dad when he moved to the front another time.

"That's why its taking a little longer," Dad said, "the water is up so high, we cain't cross."

I wondered why we hadn't stopped and build a fire. As always, Dad had his ax stuck down the collar of his hunting coat, with the blade resting

113

against the back of his head. I was sure we could have found something in all these woods that would burn. Still and all, I didn't worry like Twidge. Dad and Reek knew how to get us home alive.

Daylight came and the snow went right on coming down. It was harder and harder to put one foot in front of the other.

Dad and Reek broke trail almost all the time, and they didn't seem to fade. I wanted to stop and rest. Time seemed to drag along. At times I felt like screaming, the world was so quiet. It came to me all the sudden that night was coming on again. If we were lost, we'd have to stop before long. I felt like my mind had gone to sleep; or it was to tired to care. I looked back to make sure Twidge was following. His eyes were set deep in his face--his face was blank--he was keeping up the best he could.

I had no idea where we were--nor how long we could last. But I trusted Dad and Reek.

Whump! Whump! I came to myself. Dad and Reek were kicking the snow off their boots on the rocks at our back door step. We had walked right by the barn and crib without me knowing we were in miles of home.

"Home early," Mama said, as we filed into the kitchen.

"Snowed," Dad said, "and we had to come out."

Two days later Dad and Reek left at daylight, going back to the camp. It had rained and melted the snow down to shoe-mouth deep. We knew they wouldn't be back until they killed enough of them hogs for our winter's meat. They didn't say anything about Twidge and me going with them. I figured Mama had made it plain to them earlier that we wouldn't be going.

I never got to ask Twidge how he liked the hunting trip; he slept two straight days. The morning after that, Mama got the neighbors to take him to the bus station.

He went back to his place, and I stayed in mine. I wondered which was better. I had learned things from being with him, and I felt he might have learned something too.

Some two years later a book came in the mail. Seems like Twidge had spent six months camping and filming animals in northern Canada. It was about how he had lived off the land, eating what he could gather at times.

There was no letter with the book and it was mostly pictures. I wondered what had made him do it. The book was called; *It'll Beat A Snowball.*

MILLER'S MILL -- The Best Day

"Confound this dag-blasted wheel!" Ceece kept cussing while he kicked at the little steel wheel rim he was trying to roll. Barefoot like he was, it's a good thing he missed. Of course, Ceece always had been a boy with a short fuse. Even the grownups knew better than to rile him if they wanted any peace and quiet.

It was just past midday on a hot Saturday. We were on our way over the high mountain that stands between Rail Cove and the big creek where the old mill stood. Saturday evening was the only time not used up by hillside farming or church.

We followed the top of Buck Snort Ridge on a little skid trail full of rocks and roots. Ceece's wheel kept hitting roots and rocks until finally it ran out of the road and down the mountain. I carried mine and listened to him. I thought of telling him that we were too old to be playing wheels, but didn't.

"I ought'a burn this plaguid ivy thicket down," Ceece said as he climbed back into the road.

"Ivy won't burn; it stays green all year long," I said.

"My dad's got a new bow saw. We cou--"

"Forget it," I said.

Most boys and a few girls had wheels. Using a wire as a guide, we rolled them everywhere we went. None of us had bicycles, and the trails we followed were too rough and narrow for our wooden wagons. Some of the boys a little older than me could make the wheels do about anything they wanted them to, even roll them up the side of a tree. I never was very good and would quit rolling if it wasn't for having to look after Ceece.

"Dag-nabbit!" Ceece yelled, as he hit a tree with the wire, bending it all out of shape.

The older boys done a good job of keeping their wires straight, down to the end where they bent it in the shape of a seven. Using the seven as a hook, you could guide your wheel around a curve. If you hooked the seven inside, it acted like a brake. The best ones were made from two welding rods braised end to end, but mine and Ceece's were common old coat hangers.

When we reached the steep bluff directly above the mill, we stopped. It was kind of a rule that the smaller boys carried the wheels and wires. The big boys climbed the tall, slim pine trees that cover this side of the ridge. Once they made it up near the top, the trees would bend under their weight. They'd catch hold of a limb from a tree below them, which would bend too. We called it riding the tops. I could do it fairly well, even better than most, but stayed behind with Ceece.

There were three boys Ceece's age carrying wheels and wires. Not Ceece, he got mad once and threw all the wheels and wires into a laurel thicket. Some we never did find. The older boys would have mopped up the ground with him if some men hadn't broke it up. Me being a little older than Ceece, I usually stayed behind to sort of look after him.

"When I get bigger, I won't go to the plaguid mill, I'll go to town," Ceece said. "They got a picture show thar."

"Their drinks ain't as cold," I said.

"Yeah, but they don't drip all over you, like them do at the mill. He keeps them in all that old creek water."

"Forget it."

In just a few minutes, the older boys were down at the creek. I could hear them yelling as the stragglers made it down. I felt cooler listening to the water tumble on its way down the rough creek, a hundred yards below.

It was as hot as only a piney ridge can get. Ceece was back up the trail cussing the weather. "Dang, I'm hot. Them big'uns will have all the really cold drinks drunk up by the time we get thar."

He came running down the trail. He handed me his wheel and bent wire. "Hold this." Then he climbed a young pine just below us. The little tree started to bend when he was barely head high, but there was no other below it. Ceece landed flat on his back in the ivy thicket.

A little farther on we could see the mill roof. The split-board shingles were weathered pale gray; nearly all were turned up on the end like sled runners. In winter snow would blow through them, but they would not leak in a rain. What stood out most about the place were the three big chimneys. One on each end and another in the center--made of soapstone and chinked with clay. The center one had two fireplaces back-to-back. Strangers marveled at how straight they had stood over the years. There was no record of who built them. The mill house itself was made of poplar logs that had been hewed flat on all sides, yet were still two feet thick. Signs covered the end that faced down the creek, most of them plugging snuff or baking powder. Some were so faded that none of the words showed through the rust. As high as a body could reach, there was carving on just about every inch of the logs. Mostly hearts with initials inside. Everybody knew where the oldest carving was and what it said. I read it out loud every time I passed. "M. W. loves D. A., August 27, 1808."

On the porch facing the road, chairs and benches lined the wall. Near the door, dry feed for cows and shorts for hogs were stacked to the roof. Cured hams in flour sacks hung from the wall plate.

"I'd throw their stinking wheels in the creek," Ceece said, as we walked across the road to the mill. Then he started arguing with the others about which wheel and wire belonged to who.

I just stood and looked at the old building a long time, wondering how many like Ceece had passed by. Only the oldest of the old-timers could remember any of the family that carried the name Miller, and none of them had run the mill. The name had stuck through the years. The owner and proprietor, as Mama called him, was Randall C. Calhound, a short, bald man of about sixty. "He wears a smile as easy as a body wears an old shoe," Mama said many a time. "His eyebrows are so bushy he seems to be looking out from under a haystack." Winter or summer, he wore a white shirt with black sleeve garters just below his elbows. The cap on his head had a visor made of some green stuff you could see through. All the other men up and down the creek wore overalls and felt hats.

As we entered the mill, old man Simms brought an armload of goods and placed them on the counter.

"That'll be hit," he said, adding a twist of homemade chewing tobacco to his jaw.

Mr. Calhound started to count, picking up each thing and placing it in a flour sack Mr. Simms had laid on the counter: "Five plus three makes eight.

Forty-five equals fifty-three. Nine for the beans gets you to sixty-two. Eleven for the cheese, now I got seventy-three." By this time, he was going so fast I couldn't keep up. It sounded like a chant--he gave a running total faster than the stores in town that had cash registers.

The total came to four dollars and seventy-three cents. Mrs. Simms pulled a five-dollar bill from her apron pocket. "Your change will be twenty-seven cents," Mr. Calhound said as soon as he saw the bill.

He took it into the back room for the change. Even if the sale was only a penny for a piece of candy, Mr. Calhound went to the back room and put the penny in a tin box. No one had ever found a mistake in his counting, and if there'd ever been one, folks would have noticed. Money was hard to come by in these mountains any day or time.

During the week, small boys would trade eggs and such for candy--all but Ceece. Ceece favored chewing tobacco. Mr. Calhound would take his knife and cut a wedge from a large plug when Ceece handed him an egg.

"Hot dang, nickel's worth of backer ain't a chaw," Ceece said as he placed the wad of Apple tobacco in his mouth.

I pointed out to Ceece that the hen's nest he'd robbed probably belonged to Mr. Calhound. After all, the chickens ran loose around the mill. The egg had come from a nest just a little ways up the creek.

"If them thar eggs is his'n he ought to brand'em," Ceece said.

We went back outside, Ceece with an orange drink in each hand.

Just down the road stood a wooden bridge. Two boys were sitting on the bridge rail playing mumblety-peg while three younger boys watched. I liked to watch Aaron Lyle. He faced a boy from up on Bug Scuffle. They could make the knives land point-down on the narrow, four-inch rail every time. We could see after a few minutes that neither one was going to miss.

"I ain't got me no fancy Jefferson bone-handle knife." Ceece started throwing rocks into the water far below. "If'en I did, I could hold my own with them fellers."

"I would drop mine off that rail into the water," I said.

"You probably would. Besides, I need another cold drink." Ceece acted like I was somehow holding him back.

"You need another yeller dope and another pie," I called after him. "Might sweeten you up."

By the time I reached the part of the mill used for a store, Ceece was digging into the big red drink box, making sure the one he picked was the coldest. He finally chose a bottle of strawberry. He held it over his head; water ran down his arm and dripped off his elbow.

Ceece popped the top but didn't wipe off the bottle with the clean white towel that always hung on the side of the box. "How you like the looks of this belly washer?" he said.

The inside of the building was mostly open. The big fireplaces reached higher than a man's head. Goods were stacked all the way to the loft. Barrels of beans, pickles, and hoop cheese sat in front of the side counter. Nail kegs supplied a place for people to sit. Flypaper strips hung from the roof beams. Some looked like they had been hung back when the mill was built.

Everything from cookware to A. A. Cutter boots could be found down near the end of the main counter. The building was cool, dark, and damp, though the breeze off the creek kept down any bad odor. It had a good smell; maybe it came from the slowly melting cheese or the leather boots.

Eight cane-bottomed chairs sat facing the huge fireplaces. I always made sure to go by there if the McTalleys were sitting by the hearth. In winter, it would be a sure bet; in summer, Saturday was the only time you could count on. Everybody called them the twins, though they were in their seventies. Because they had never married, I figured.

They were rich by our standards in land and cattle. They owned what bottomland there was along the creek and they had cattle and hogs that ranged in the mountains. Whenever a twenty-dollar bill came through the store, they would argue over who got to give change for it.

"Once a dollar gets salted down in a breast pocket of their overalls, you'll never see it again," I had heard people say many a time.

Elbert was tall and lanky and smoked a pipe. Delbert was short and squatty--a tobacco twist and snuff man. They were always together and always arguing. Folks say in their younger days that they had fistfights that went from morning to night. Then they would start back in the next morning, right where they left off.

"When one of them gets a cold, the other sneezes," my uncle Earl allowed. "They got all the money in the world and their clothes look like they robbed a scarecrow."

I looked over toward the fireplaces. The twins were sitting there alone, each facing a fireplace. I could see both of them, but with the big hearths between them, they couldn't see each other.

Ceece pinched me on the arm as we came near. "They're at it again."

We sat down on nail kegs so we could listen. I could smell the dried cow manure that covered their unlaced brogans. Each of them had only one overall gallows fastened--for some reason they always unfastened one when the argument got heated up. Delbert was so heavy he couldn't fasten the side flap. It looked like the things would fall off if he stood up.

Ceece swung both arms over his head, like he was using a pitchfork. We both snickered. I looked at the faded blue shirts the twins wore, at the sweat circles under their armpits.

"Them clothes is so ragged they use a pitchfork to put'em on with," Ceece said.

Delbert loaded his lip with snuff, then broke off a piece of tobacco twist and filled his jaw. Elbert pitched the remainder of a pickled pig's foot into the ashes. Some folks claimed that's all he ate. He walked over to the counter and brought back the whole jar of pig's feet. I figured this had to be a humdinger of an argument.

"I heard you a'talkin to Widder Smith day a'fore yesterday," Elbert said, "when she brung over them tater cakes for you. She had on so much toilet water I could smell her long before I seed her. Had so much of that jet oil on her hair it run down her neck and turned her collar black."

Delbert packed a little more snuff in his lip before he answered. He spat into the ashes, and a little of the juice landed on his overall bib. "When she asked you, 'How do you take your coffee, Elbert?' you said, 'A little maiden's cream and two cubes of sugar.' You always drunk your coffee black, same as me. I ought to know. I've been cooking for you for pert-near sixty years or longer."

"Tain't so, I can cook as well as you," Elbert said as he took another nibble off a pig's foot.

"Course, a body would have to clean the hog grease off the skillet first."

Delbert spat into the ashes with enough force to split a rock. "Why, I wouldn't eat an egg you gathered. Good-ness sakes alive! Neither would I eat a walnut you hulled. You've et them darn pickled pig's feet til your brain is pickled."

Elbert was busy nibbling and trying to light his pipe at the same time. He looked like he might blow up any minute. Delbert leaned back, grinning; his chin was brown from tobacco juice.

I followed Ceece over to the mill works. We could always go back if the ruckus got going good again.

It was cool back near the rear wall 'cause the water wheel was only inches outside the wall. Part of the millpond ran up under that side of the building. The big locust driveshaft was still. The millstones sat quiet and cold. I stood and looked over the well-worn parts. Some of the corn hoppers were over a hundred and fifty years old. You could smell the age of the wood.

A log truck came down the creek and pulled into the parking lot. An old farmer pitched a sack of corn onto the porch, then walked into the mill. "You grind this turn of corn fur me?" he asked, seeing Mr. Calhound behind the counter.

"Yes sir. Be proud to."

"I need to carry this tan bark on to town," the farmer said. "Be back di-rectly."

"I'll have it waiting when you come back through. Haven't seen anyone from up around the Meadow's Bald all week--how's all the folks up your way?"

It was plain that Mr. Calhound was being his uncommonly friendly self, and that the old farmer wasn't used to being talked to so polite like.

"Fair-to-middlin," the farmer said, then climbed back into the old truck.

"Further they live up the creek, the less they talk," Mr. Calhound said.

I picked up the sack of corn and followed Mr. Calhound back to the mill works. He stepped over to a small window and spoke to the boys climbing the water wheel. "I've got to grind this turn of corn, so keep the little ones clear of the wheel." Mr. Calhound talked to the boys with the same respect he showed grownups. "Carl, when everybody's clear, will you start the wheel?"

"He won't let me start the plaguid thing," Ceece muttered. "Hit's always the big'uns who get to do everything."

We poured the grain into the shaker box. "Look at how little this corn is," I said, hoping to sidetrack him from the head of steam he was building up.

"Nothing but a bunch of nubbins," he said, as if I didn't know it already. "That's all that grows way back up on the creek."

Carl climbed up to the millrace. It was easy to change the flow of the water. A wore-out millstone hanging on the end of a white oak pole acted as a counterweight. With one hand, Carl moved the heavy wooden gate from one opening in the flume to the other. By the time the water started the giant wheel moving, he'd come through the small door at the top of the wheel. In winter or when he was alone, the miller could control the gate without getting wet.

By the time the wore-out millstone stopped swinging on the log chain, the wooden shaft had commenced to turn. It squeaked like a dead limb in the wind as it started the huge stone.

The feed hopper began to shake. With all the slack taken up, the millstones started grinding. The smell of warm corn meal soon filled the air around where we stood. Chaff blew toward the small open window.

Mr. Calhound stood by the small flume that carried the meal down to a bin. He kept feeling the meal between his thumb and forefinger. If it was not to his liking, he used the other hand to tighten or let off on the leather thong that controls the flow of corn. Too fine and he let the corn flow into the mill faster; too coarse, and he slowed the flow down so the corn spent more time between the stones. When he got it just right, he grabbed a wooden scoop.

Nine scoops went into the farmer's flour sack, the tenth into the miller's barrel.

"This smell is making me hongry," Ceece said as we watched the last corn spill into the hopper.

We walked back outside. You had to be careful while crossing the parking lot barefooted. Bottle caps covered the ground. Some were bright and shiny; others were brown with rust. I could read the words on some. Nu-grape and Orange seemed to be favorites, but others had been there so long that they were just little circles of rust. They did keep the mud down in the parking space, but they tore up bare feet. In places, they were several inches thick, and Ceece was adding to them; he stood on the porch with a soft drink in each hand.

Alone at one end of the porch sat Ty Riddle from up on Burnt Dam Branch. Right at seven feet, he was the tallest man in these parts. He had little to say to anyone and had never owned a riding horse or car. You were apt to see him walking anywhere within fifty miles of his home. Some said he could never find a horse that could keep up with him. Seeing his long loping gait, you could believe it. It was easy to spot him by the big black umbrella he carried, winter or summer, rain or shine.

"Why do you carry that umbrella all the time?" strangers asked him from time to time.

"Hit keeps me dry when it rains or snows--slows the cold north wind--gives me shade from the hot summer sun. A man who's raised twenty kids needs to take care of hisself."

His answer might not make sense to strangers, but we all knew his next words were true. "Ten boys. Ten girls. With three sets of twins."

Ty sat for a few minutes before stepping down off the high porch. He went up the road almost in a trot.

"Quire as a three-dollar bill," Ceece said, when Ty was out of sight.

At the north end of the mill stood a buckeye tree, so big its shade covered at least a half an acre. A dozen or more men were passing the time pitching horseshoes in the shade.

"Let's do something to make them mad," Ceece said.

"Them men wouldn't let you play if you begged like a pup," I said to Ceece as we walked over.

"I'll double-dog-dare you to pick a fight," Ceece Said.

"Shut up!" I said.

We watched them for about an hour. They wouldn't let us take a turn, which made Ceece so mad he cussed up a storm under his breath.

"Look at it this way," I said. "They throw at least two ringers out of four pitches. The only way we can throw one is pure luck. We wouldn't get to pitch but once til we got beat."

"Holy cow, whose side you on anyway? Maybe we'd both get lucky at the same time--if'en they'd only let us pitch."

I could see he wasn't anywhere near ready to let it go. Besides, he had rested up from the trip and wanted to start a racket.

"Remember that fit you had a while back?" I asked him. "You know, when you swore til you was blue that your leaner was worth more than two ringers? They ain't even studying about letting you play."

He started cussing again, so I gave up. As I walked away for a few minutes, I heard the two best pitchers, Ledbetter and Shope, telling him the same thing, in almost the same words. One said it stronger and the others a-men'd it.

A bunch of little kids were under the porch playing cars with empty thread spools. The mounds of earth, dry for over a hundred years, made a fine place to play in the dirt. Thousands of little roads tracked the dirt and sand.

Ceece had to hunker down to scoot under the floor. He tore up their roads as he crawled around, but they gave him room without causing a fuss. No telling how long he would've stayed under there if he hadn't been so big he had to fold like a pocket book just to move about.

"Come on," I said as I brushed the dirt from his clothes. "I reckon we've out-grown playing cars."

We went back inside the mill just as the wheel was making its last turn. Once the water flow had been changed, the bulk of the water spilled out of the gate on the side of the spillway. The noise died down as the giant wheel came to rest and the millstones, with a final squeak, settled together. I touched the top of the stone: it was warm and moist. No wonder Mama wouldn't use cornmeal ground on a motor-driven mill.

Elbert and Delbert were at it again.

"I like to kill hogs when the signs are in the feet," Delbert was saying. "Hit's the best time."

"Everybody with the sense God gave a goose knows the best time to kill hogs is when the weather is cold," Elbert fired back. "That way the meat don't spile."

"How do you know? You only eat them stinking pickled pig's feet." Delbert spat with the speed of a bullet. "Lordy. Bacon fry up in a little curl, onliest thing fit to eat is the bilin pieces. Red-eye gravy tastes like coffee."

"Plant when the signs are in the body, build fence when the signs are in the legs. Lordy, de-horn a calf when the signs are in the head and hit'll bleed to death. I seed that proved."

Elbert had his pipe and tobacco pouch in one hand and a pig's foot in the other, clearly about to get earnest with the argument. I had heard it all many times before. Any minute, he'd be quoting scripture to prove his point.

"Hit's in the Good Book," I heard him say as I walked away.

I left the twins and walked over to where Mr. Calhound and Thad Weaver were playing checkers. They were the best players in the mountains, and by the long-faced looks, I could tell they were butting heads for all they were worth. One would move a bottle cap, and then wait while the other studied. On the old wooden board, faded by years of use, it was hard to tell where some squares left off and others started.

A game sometimes lasted for an hour or better. This one looked to be getting down to the end. Mr. Calhound got a checker up on Thad.

"That's the game--I give," Thad said. "No body can beat you with one less checker."

"You're right," Mr. Calhound said as he set the board back up. He placed the checkers on their squares in five seconds. "Cain't beat you that way neither."

Someone behind me said, "I believe if the place caught fire, them two wouldn't know it til the checker board burnt up."

"I'd not give up because I had one less checker," Ceece said. "No-sir-ee!"

"I don't think you have any notion how they play the game," I said.

"I'm of a mind to go find me a fight," Ceece said.

I wandered back outside, then down to the millpond. Over on the far side, three women were fishing. No kids were swimming; the pond was as still as a mirror. I knew it was full of big trout, but nobody could catch them--all the good fly fishermen knew it was a lost cause. We all figured Mr. Calhound had them trained. Every once in a while, usually after a storm, one would bite-- probably one that had washed over the spillway or made its way up the river.

All of a sudden, one of the women got a bite. This set them all to jabbering. I walked around the pond, puzzled to know what kind of fish she'd hooked. I thought it was a big minnow or maybe a red horse. When I got closer, I saw it was a bluegill. A big one, the size of a man's hand. She pulled it to the bank and strung it on a forked stick. Besides the bluegill, there were two horny heads, about five inches long.

Something moved up on the hill above them. A deer? Then I saw her. The prettiest girl I had ever laid eyes on was sitting under a big hemlock tree with her feet in a spring branch. I closed my eyes and pinched my arm. I had to be dreaming, and sure enough, when I looked again I didn't see her.

My heart felt like a rock, but I hurried toward the hemlock tree anyway. I'd walked only a few yards before I saw her again. She wore a simple brown dress and a necklace of clay beads. Her skin was the color of old copper and looked just as smooth. Her eyes were the same rich black as her hair. Most girls have one or two good traits, but she didn't have one that wasn't. She sat as still as a fawn, among the rough rocks and burly hemlocks.

"Where did you come from?" The words sounded like I'd gone crazy.

"Over on the Tallahala River--a place called Terrapin Cove. Just above Big Sandy, if you know that section?"

Her teeth shined like wet flint when she talked. Her voice was sweet and low.

"I know where Terrapin Cove is." The words came out without me making a fool of myself.

She stood up. My heart almost stopped. Was she about to leave? Had she got put off with my questions? I tried hard to say something else but my mouth wouldn't work right.

Then she sat back down, farther over on the rock. She smiled. I sat down on the moss-covered rock next to her. I had the urge to touch her, only, I was afraid she would go away like a ghost or a puff of smoke if I did.

We talked for a good while. "What is your name?" she said.

"Quill. Quill Vance." It looked like I was going to stutter in spite of myself. "What's yours?"

"La'Homa Swimmer. I'm staying with Aunt Nellie Potter, up on Roaring Fork Creek."

We talked on. I didn't stutter any more for she was easy to talk to. I found out she was seventeen and that scared me a little. She didn't ask my age as I tried to count the months that I was younger than she was. Right at twenty, I was figuring when she spoke. "Let's go for a walk."

She led the way. I was shocked at how smooth she moved as we made our way up the rough spring branch. It sure was more fun to travel with her than with Ceece. We made a loop toward the ridge top, and she stopped at the crest.

"Down there is where Aunt Nellie lives."

"I know the place." I got my breath. "Heck, I know everybody that lives up on Roaring Fork Creek. Matter of fact, I helped Nellie get her winter's wood last year."

She moved through the thick laurel like a deer, until I grabbed her hand. "Don't go through there. Poison ivy." I pointed at the little three-leaf plants covering the ground.

"Poison ivy don't bother me," she said, walking bare-foot through the patch. "Only you boys get broke out all over."

"Shoot, I knew poison ivy didn't bother you. It don't me neither, much." I hurried around to the other side, feeling like a fool. When I got there, she

136

took my hand and gave it a tight squeeze. I felt a feeling of warmth go all over me. Boy, did I want to touch her again.

"Will you let me walk you home later?"

"Maybe. It depends. I'll have to ask Aunt Nellie."

When we got back to the millpond, the women were resetting their fishing poles. While La'Homa went to talk to her aunt I stood on a rock, moving my feet like I was on pins and needles. The women most likely thought the rock was hot. From time to time, they'd looked my way and laugh. They talked on and on. Generally, I could understand what was being said well enough, but they were talking fast and with their hands. It was plain as day they didn't want me to know something, or else they were teasing me. I wished they would hurry.

La'Homa's face, as she came toward me, was like a piece of stone. Then a big smile spread across her lips. "It's all right with her; she just wants us not to make it too late. She wants us to start home by full dark, anyway."

We walked back toward the mill, holding hands. My feelings had been so up and down my knees were weak: my legs felt wobbly. I needed to sit down. Then again, I wanted to show her off to the people around the mill. I hoped the sun would never go down.

"Who won the checker game?" I asked Thad Weaver, who was sitting on the top boulder that served as an end step to the porch.

"About like common," he said. "We each won three games, then we settled down and tied eight straight."

We went into the mill. I bought La'Homa a soft drink, and Mr. Calhound winked at me when he brought the change.

The McTalley brothers were still sitting at the fireplaces. "I know for a fact that a white mule is easier to keep than a brown, or black, for that matter," Elbert said.

Delbert shook his head. "A white mule will live to be a hundred just to kick your head off. Me, I like a listed mule."

They both started talking at once, neither willing to stop so he could hear the other, until they saw La'Homa. Then they stopped talking. They stared at her. I reckon the sight of her must of brought back memories, for they were quiet for several seconds. Then they started right back up again arguing about the weather.

Mr. Calhound had moved to the porch, carrying his clippers and comb. He would cut hair any time of the day if he wasn't busy. On Saturdays, he started at 3:00. There, big as life, stood Ceece, trying to hog the line.

"Get me a soup bowl, I want to cut Ceece's hair," one of the horseshoe pitchers said, "his head need croppin."

"Naw, you won't. I don't want no soup-bowl haircut!" Ceece made so much noise I couldn't hear the waterfalls. He ranted and raved and said a hundred times, "You won't put no blame bowl on my head."

"Not for your head," the man said. "To cover your mouth with."

All the people laughed, which got Ceece's goat. Most times, he carried on like he was dying, but this time he didn't even raise a fuss when the clippers pinched him on the neck.

We heard a big log truck coming up the creek, bouncing real slow over the boulders in the road. It pulled in beside the gas pump. All the haircuts were finished, and Mr. Calhound held a little girl in his lap. She was fast asleep.

"What can I help you with?" Mr. Calhound asked, as he laid the little girl down real careful.

"Give me two dollars' worth of gas, and I need a quart of lamp oil in this here can."

It was the farmer who had brought the corn earlier. He lived way up on the head of Meadows Creek.

Mr. Calhound took the spouted tin can and filled it with oil, then turned the crank handle on the gas pump. Gasoline rose in the glass bubble way up on top of the pump. He stopped when the gas reached the ten-gallon mark, took the hose down and placed it in the truck gas tank. It gurgled as it drained into the truck.

Mr. Calhound spoke to the woman in the cab. She didn't say a word, just shook her head once. He turned and went back into the mill.

There were two small boys, not talking, not moving, in the truck cab. The woman didn't move either. I could tell that some kind of bowl had been used as a guide to cut the boys' hair.

We were poor by any standard, but not compared to these people. Living was hard way up on the Meadows.

I looked at La'Homa. Her face was sober, almost sad.   I was afraid Ceece would say something about the boys' haircuts. My mind was made up to hit him if he did, but he just stared at them for a long time before he spoke.

"They gotta be scrunched to death in thar," Ceece said. "Look, did you see them hair cu--"

I put my hand over his mouth, and gave him the hard look. He started to say something and I whispered in his face. "You say one word and I'll bust your nose for you."

He jerked loose and walked away. I saw him looking at rocks to throw at me; but he only looked back like I'd stole something from him.

The old farmer came out of the mill carrying a small cardboard box under his arm. It held coffee, soda, sugar, salt, and baking powder: what my Aunt Nica called the table staples. He placed the box on the truck bed, took his tire chains and wedged it firmly against the cab.

He went back into the mill and came out with the cornmeal, which he flung up on the truck bed beside the box. I couldn't help noticing his shoes; mason-jar rubbers around his foot held the soles on.

As the truck started, Mr. Calhound ran down the steps, a small poke of candy in his hand. He jumped up on the running board and passed it through the window.

Ceece looked around as if he was lost, saw I was holding La'Homa's hand, and came tearing over to where we stood. "Is she blind?"

"Sure is," I said. I figured he'd tell me she didn't need leading if I said no. She put on an act for him, held my hand tight and let me lead her several steps. Ceece backed up like he thought she might run over him.

"When are we going home?" he said.

I didn't even grin. "It's going to be late. You see, Somebody has to walk this poor blind girl home."

"Where she live?"

"Head of the creek, up near the old Ranson Place." I said it quick hoping he would take it for the truth.

"Why, that, that place is haunted," Ceece said. "There's haints everywhere. Besides, the woods is

141

full of varmints and a body cain't hear 'em for the blamed creek. I ain't going up thar after dark!"

It made me proud that Ceece feared something I didn't. Proud, and at the same time a little sorry for him.

"Ceece, It's four hours before dark."

I led the way to the back of the mill house, up above the wheel, where hardly anyone ever went. The mill wasn't running but the noise from the water tumbling fifty feet to the rocks below was deafening. La'Homa was still playing blind as we walked between the big boulders.

All at once she stopped and put both arms around my neck and kissed me full in the mouth. My first kiss. The only kisses I'd ever had were cheek pecks from my family, mostly my sisters, which didn't count. La'Homa's were like nothing I had ever tasted: kinda like burnt sugar. Only better. When I hugged her, she seemed to kind of melt in my arms. So little, so fragile, yet so full of life. She moaned way down as we kissed again. I never knew older girls were this much fun.

"Let's carve our initials on a log," I said while we caught our breaths. She lead the way back to the front of the mill. I wanted the carving to be where everyone could see it.

"No." She pointed to a place between two bear hides hanging on the log wall.

It looked like I was as dumb as a stump full of granddaddy spiders. Many old-timers didn't like their pictures taken or symbols made of them. My grandpa was like that. I felt like a fool until I thought about what it meant for her to let me carve it anywhere.

Reaching in my pocket, I took out my knife and made a motion like I was going to carve a heart as big as two logs' width. She shook her head. I held my hands about six inches apart, and she widened them to the width of one log.

When I finished the heart was about a foot high. She pointed to where to put my initials up near the top, a plus mark in the center, then her initials at the bottom.

We started kissing something awful. I could tell this was likely to become my favorite thing to do. When we finished, she gave me a smile so sweet. I kissed her again. More times than I could count.

Mama had warned me not to mess around with girls that might be some of our kin. I tried to recall were it is that all our folks live over that way, but my mind wouldn't work fast. We've got a lot of kin living in the Tallalhala section but at least none of them are named Swimmer. Anyhow, that wasn't no time to be thinking on things like that; it was a time to be courting.

My legs were so weak I couldn't hardly walk. We went back to the road side of the mill where Ceece was sitting in a pile of rich pine shavings. He was working like a beaver, sticking little slivers of pine in a split knot.

"What are you doing?" I said.

"Making me some pine-knot torches."

Ceece didn't look up, so he never noticed that La'Homa had stopped acting like she was blind. He finished one torch and started another. Most of the time I felt put out with him, but now I only felt sad. He was purely afraid of the dark.

One of the first things Mama taught us was not to make fun of a person's fears or try to make them worse. They could hurt themselves or somebody else. It's sort of like chasing a coward; it's all right to run after him, but you better not catch him. If you do, he's apt to hurt you real bad.

I saw Elmo Garrett and his pregnant wife loading their supplies in flour sacks. They lived above us, at the head of the cove. I went over and asked Elmo if he would let Ceece walk home with them. "He can help tote your load," I added.

"Fine with me."

I walked over to Ceece. "They need you to walk home with them and help carry their things and stuff." He grinned like somebody had just given him a new red wagon. He grabbed up a hand full of torches in his right hand and a sack of flour under the other arm.

"Come on, Ceece. The sun is still shined up on the high tops." I tossed some of the torches across the road. "There'll be some music after a while."

144

He still seemed to be in a god-awful hurry. Without looking at me, he swung the flour sack over his shoulder and headed out down the road. Elmo gave me a funny look, then they followed Ceece.

By then, the summer breezes had died down. The horseshoe game had ended. The men had gone home to tend their stock. As the shadows grew longer, many of the old people headed home. The women were gone from the pond.

Thirty minutes later a car rounded the bend above the mill. It was red. I had thought all cars were black. Inside were two boys and two girls about my age or a year or so older. I read the name on the front of the car: Whippet Roadster. The boys were wearing little billed driving caps. The driver even had on a pair of white gloves. Both girls stood up and waved as they passed. One had long, blond hair; the other one had short, auburn-colored hair. We could tell they were showing off, standing up so the whole world could see they were pretty.

"Them girls act too bigity and feisty," Elbert McTalley said after they passed.

"I wouldn't trade that little black-haired girl with Quill, for a cow pasture full like'em," Delbert added.

"Me neither," Mr. Calhound said in the loudest voice I'd ever heard him use. "Not if they throwed in a whole fleet of them red cars. That's the first thing I've ever heard you and McTalley agree on." He went into the mill and brought out an old hog's head banjo. All of us moved closer. "A little racket ought'a liven up this place." He put his foot on a nail keg and commenced to play.

"Let's go check on our carving," I said after La'Homa and I had listened to a few songs. I felt ten feet tall.

Back at the carving, we kissed til my lips were sore. She let me feel of her breasts, cupping her hand over mine. I didn't know what this meant but it felt like I'd found something that would make me happy for the rest of my days. The buttons on the end were nothing like what I have seen when women feed their babies. They were no bigger than a half-grown blackberry--soft in some ways but got bigger and harder all the time. When I brushed them lightly through her clothes, they stood out like they were asking for more--like they were trying to help me feel of them. It hurt from the hardness bound up by my britches. I wanted to move it, but was afraid that would scare her and she would make me stop. Everything moved so fast and so slow--It was hard to tell what to do. I wrapped my free arm around her and pulled her tight against me. She seemed to melt like butter against my body. At first I thought I might be hurting her, but she only moaned like a kitten and kissed me, running her tongue over my teeth. The only thing that came anyway near close to tasting that good was ice cream. My head spun. My heart beat faster than a flutter mill. I must be in love.

I hadn't noticed the music coming from the road side of the mill until she straightened her clothes and hair. "Let's go listen to the music and cool off for a spell."

I knew without seeing them that the Travis brothers had joined Mr. Calhound. The crowd got bigger. There was hand clapping and dancing, laughing and singing. We left the carving and went back to the front of the mill.

All three of the Travis brothers made music. Darrell played the fiddle; Corley played guitar and sang. Peanut, the youngest and smallest, played the base and the harmonica. I had never heard what his given name was. Out and about in public, the brothers were quiet, almost timid-like. None of them talked much, and when they did talk; it was in a voice barely louder than a whisper. But while they had anything with wire strings in their hands, they sang loud. The music bounced off the steep sides of the valley, rocking it like a thunderstorm.

"We better start for home," La'Homa said after we'd listened for about an hour.

On the porch, old folks had left and young ones had taken their place. Many couples held hands, and we sat down with them for maybe a half an hour. Tye Riddle had come back and was dancing by himself to every tune, just out of the light of the coal oil lanterns. A few of the couples danced in the roadway. None of them could hold a light to Tye Riddle.

"He'll be dancing when they get around to playing 'Amazing Grace,'" La'Homa whispered in my ear.

I laughed. Not only was she beautiful, she was funny. I felt better than any time I could remember.

"Do you know what his wife does--mostly?" She said.

At first, I thought of her cooking and canning. Then, I thought of Tye Riddle's twenty children. "Have babies, so I've heard."

"Have babies, make moccasins, have more babies and make more moccasins. If she'd stop one, the other would stop."

"Maybe she don't know what causes babies," I said. This being the first time I had ever talked to a girl about babies, I was wondering how she'd take it.

She turned and started walking up the creek road. I wanted to talk about babies, but I held her hand and walked along feeling better than good. Our being in a hurry didn't keep us from stopping and kissing every hundred yards or so. We ran for a ways, then stopped and kissed some more. I had never done anything in my whole life that felt so good. The night was warm. La'Homa was soft and cuddly. Once she let me feel of her breasts and I got the top of her dress open enough to see the left one. I wanted to touch it with my tongue so bad it hurt.

"No, not now," She said.

If we walked slow enough it would take until daybreak to reach Nellie's house, I thought to myself. It stood almost in the road but sat twenty feet above it. We stopped fifty feet before we reached the house and sat down on a sycamore log between the road and creek. She put her arms around my neck before I could say a word. Her tongue flickered around the inside my mouth. Her breath was warmer than before. The taste was the same but somehow it was much stronger.

I put my hand on her leg just above the knee. Her leg was firm and well shaped but as my hand rubbed the inside of her thigh, her skin felt soft--it was like a baby's. I worked my hand up slow. It felt hotter than anything that hadn't burnt me. My hand was only inches away from where I wanted it to be.

Both her hands grabbed mine at the same time. "No. No, don't touch that."

I thought she was mad for what I had tried to do. I'd heard girls slapped your jaws but it would be worth a good slap if she'd let me touch her there. After a few minutes she let me kiss her. We kissed again and again; ever time it was better. By then, I had her right breast uncovered and she let me put my mouth on the button. She trembled and shuddered, as it grew firmer and sweeter. I tried one more time to feel between her legs but she stopped me before my hand made its way much above her knee. She made it plain that I wasn't gonna touch her between her legs again. La'Homa let me know how far I could go without a harsh word or a slap. I worked as hard as I could on the kissing and playing with her buttons. Her whole body was as soft as potter's clay, and I was having so much fun I pinched my arm to make sure I wasn't dreaming. If this weren't love it was the next best thing.

A dim light flickered on and off in the house as if someone had lit a lamp and put it out. "I've got to go in now," La'Homa said. She led me up some steep steps and across a narrow yard to more steps reaching up to the porch. The inside of the house was dark and quiet. We stood on the porch and must have kissed until well after midnight. We might have kissed til morning if a faint noise from inside the house had not startled us.

"You have to go," La'Homa said. "She'll be mad if I don't come in now."

She gave me one longer kiss, then slipped inside the door.

While we'd been doing all that kissing, a late night storm had rolled in. By the time I left Nellie's house, the sky had become as dark as a cave. I missed the steps and fell headfirst out in the yard, landing on my hands and knees.

Then, I was totally turned around. I mistook a gap in the hedge for the steps leading down to the road. Down over the bank I went. This time I landed on my face. I got up; glad nobody had seen the falls. When I got straightened out on which way the road ran, I heard Nellie's low laugh coming from the house.

I knew La'Homa had teased me. "Still, I'd do it all over again right now if I knew I'd fall into the creek and drown," I said out loud.

Lightning helped me find my way down the creek road. Any other time, traveling in a dark storm would scare me to death, but I paid it no mind.

When I reached the mill, the rain came down in sheets. The old building seemed to take on more age than I had noticed before. Though my legs didn't feel weak anymore, I sat on the porch for a few minutes, as happy as I had ever been in my life.

I found one of Ceece's torches--the ones I'd thrown into the bushes across the road--and lit it. I would need the light for sure on the trail crossing Buck Snort Ridge. About the time I started down into the cove, I thought about my wheel and wire. The best I could remember, they were still in the bushes across from the mill. Maybe some little kid would find them and have some fun. For me, they had lost their charm.

PERD'S BIRD -- The Oldest Sport

"I know where we can come up with us some game chickens," Ceece said, hanging the gourd back on the hemlock limb.

"How much?" I said.

Ceece picked up his hoe and looked at the blade; he studied the edge for a spell, like he was holding back something that nobody else had figured. With his right thumb, he felt of the hoe's edge like it was a razor. A grin came over his face as he turned to me. "For free, I tell you."

"You're the very one that rocked my hog." I said, taking a long whetrock from my hip pocket and pointing it in his face. "I ain't about to take no thrashin for helpin you steal chickens."

Backing up two steps, Ceece took a file from his pocket and raked it across his hoe the wrong way; it made a screeching sound that hurt my ears. "Well, I done and got me two fine fighting cocks."

I knew that the new barn built over on Smokerise was a chicken-fighting place. However, I had never been there. Every Saturday morning

Reek came down out of the cove with a rooster under his arm. He never stopped at our house. Mama would not hold to any part of chicken fighting. She would have Dad flog me like a setting hen if she heard about me being there. If she had any notion that I would steal a chicken, she'd run me off from home as sure as God looks after drunks and young'uns.

"Oh, everything is on the up and up."

"Are you sure? You didn't steal'em?" I said. "We've done some things that if Dad knew about, he'd take his razor strop to us. If he caught me stealing chickens, he'd tan my hide and nail it on the barn door."

Before Ceece could answer, Dad and Reek came down out of the cornfield. Dad drove the mule and Reek carried the cultivator plow on his shoulder.

Ceece was still trying to sharpen his hoe. It made a gosh-awful noise. He stopped when Reek got near the spring. "Reek, would you help me get my rooster ready to fight."

"Shaw, where'd you get a gamecock?"

"I got me two Roundheads and a Gray Hackle."

"Shaw, you want'a swap'um."

"Reek don't know nothing about conditioning chickens." Dad had walked up. "But he'll trade."

"Shaw, a body's got to feed'em all kinds of yerbs and sich. A little gun powder don't hurt nary a bit."

"Yeah," Dad said, "all Reek ever feeds his is a little cracked corn now and again, when he's got it. He once sold a fellow from aways off a half-grown bantam rooster for a proven gamecock."

A broad smile came over Reek's face, almost choking him on his snuff. He pushed his old black hat back on his bald head. "That little rooster was one fightin fool."

"Reek," Dad said, "you won't do."

"Shaw, I'll tell a man."

Dad looked over to where we stood. "You two hands need to go up there and finish hoeing them last rows. The ones up against the timber."

"Won't grow nothin but nubbins," Ceece said.

Dad reached up and pulled the hoe down from the hemlock limb where Ceece had just hung it. He pointed with the hoe handle toward the hillside. I knew the talking was over. Ceece followed me as we climbed back to the top edge of the field. It took a spell before we caught our breath, then Ceece never quit talking about chickens. "Come Saturday I'll get me a couple more roosters. You can come along; we'll go halvers."

We had plenty of chickens, but none of them were the fighting kind. Mama put some dominicker eggs under a bantam hen. She claimed bantams made the best mothers if there were foxes around.

We had guinea fowl running all over the place. Mama said we'd eat guinea eggs if the chickens stopped laying, but it never came to that.

"Well, I'll go with you, but if there's any chicken stealin in it, Mama will have Dad thrash me. Then I'll give you one."

Ceece came to the house Saturday morning almost before daybreak. Most of the time he got there about the time Mama had breakfast ready, and he stayed until we ate dinner. This time he grabbed a cold biscuit out of the warmer, bit off one corner, and headed for the door. "Boy, come on, we're a wasting time. They're having a derby today."

"What's a derby?" I said. "That's a hat."

"Not in the world of us cock fighters it ain't. It's like the granddaddy of all chicken fights. A lot of birds will fight til just one is the winner. Big money on them."

I jerked on my boots and caught up with him down by the spring. He held an old shoebox under his right arm. "What's the rush," I said, "we can be the other side of Many Forks in two hours. What'cha got in that old shoebox?"

Ceece switched arms with the box like there was gold inside and he didn't want me to know. He always carried his pockets full of junk, which made his britches look like a sack full of rat nests.

Ceece headed down the road without saying a word. I got tickled following him--always before he had followed me, most times making every step I did.

"Slow down," I said. "Your walking like your ass is on fire."

The new tin on the roof shined as the sun rose over the Thunderbird Mountains. Otherwise, the barn looked as calm as a picture in a book.

"You lied to me," I said, "there's not a soul in sight. You mean to steal some chickens before anybody shows up."

Ceece backed up two steps and held his free hand up "No. No. We'll watch and see what they bring, at's all."

I sat on a pine pole beside the trail and watched the barn. Along about midmorning, a truck came up the road with the bed full of chicken coops. Ceece jumped up like ants had stung him on the rump.

A big man got out of the truck. He had on the biggest hat with the widest brim I ever saw. A short fat woman got out of the other side of the truck. She held a folded apron in her hand.

"Who are they?" I said.

"Why, that there's the pit boss--that's who. He runs the place."

"Who's the woman, then?"

"That's his wife. She does the cookin."

I couldn't see no way Ceece could steal chickens from that big fellow. He had to weigh over three hundred pounds. I saw a gun stuck in his britches pocket.

Ceece stood and stared at the barn, like all kinds of things were taking place down there. Once the man and woman went into the barn, everything was still again.

I found me a piece of flint and whacked away, trying to make an arrowhead. "Here," I said, handing him a piece of flint about the size of my fist. "Make yourself an arrowhead."

Ceece took it and held it in his hand for a long time. He didn't take his eyes off the barn. Then he threw the flint down the bank. I had never seen him act so set on anything.

By the time the sun got a quarter-high above the ridge, trucks and wagons came into sight, winding their way up the creek road. A few minutes later, the grass in front of the barn was near about full.

"Let's move down closer," Ceece said, "I want to see what-in-all they brung."

"I want to eat," I said, throwing down the sorry arrowheads I'd made.

"We'll eat directly; they even got a kitchen in the place."

More trucks and wagons parked in the grass as we slid off the bank into the flat. Most had homemade chicken coops tied on the back.

"Look-ee here," Ceece said, pointing to a rooster perched on the running board of a log truck. "Ain't he one fine Roundhead."

I looked the chicken over close. It did have long black feathers on its tail, and the head and neck

157

were reddish orange. Its head was shaped like all the other chickens I'd ever seen.

"That chicken's head is shaped like all the other chickens I've ever seen," I said, knowing Ceece wouldn't answer. His mind was lost in study of a gray rooster on the end gate of a wagon. He looked at every chicken and coop we passed as if he had money to buy some of them.

I counted over thirty roosters tied to trucks or wagons. They all had a leather band around their leg, laced up like a boot, with a rawhide thong tied to it. The other end of the thong was tied to whatever the chicken sat on.

Some people had hens in wire boxes sitting on the ground. Other folks had eggs in straw in the wagon beds.

I could hear bartering going on from time to time. Ceece listened and mumbled to himself. It sounded like he knew all there was to know about chickens. I'd have felt better if I'd stayed at home. It bothered me when he talked to himself.

I looked back at Ceece as I made my way into the barn. He worm-worked his way between the trucks and wagons, studying every chicken as he went.

Inside the building, it didn't look like a barn at all. There was not a bale of hay or stable in the whole place. Sawmill slab seats reached all the way to the rafters. A circle in the center of the building had a wall around it about a foot high. Where the chicken fights took place, I figured.

The faint odor of frying grease and coffee came from behind the seats. My stomach tried to eat my backbone. I found the woman from the first truck cooking, working like a beaver. The fatback smoldering on top of the stove made my eyes and mouth water at the same time.

"Could I have a biscuit and a piece of that hog meat?" I said.

The woman slid a piece of pork into a big cat-head biscuit. She handed it to me without looking my way. Her right hand scooped up the dime I'd dropped and put it in a tin box.

"What time do they start?" I said.

"In a little over an hour," She said, wiping her hands on her flour-covered apron.

I took the biscuit and walked out behind the barn. There was a trail leading up the spring branch. Along the way, there were three jugs hidden against the branch bank. By walking way up on the bank, I made sure I didn't go close to either one. Whoever owned the liquor might be watching.

I sat down under the big ash tree by the spring and watched more trucks and wagons park in the field. Every few minutes someone would sneak up the branch and drink from one of the jars.

It took a lot of spring water to kill the taste of all the salt in the fatback. Feeling full and rested, I laid down on the mossy ground and watched Reek out in the yard, spitting snuff and talking a mile a minute. Both his hands were full of pocketknives. When the spring water had cooled the burning in my belly, I went in the back door of the barn so Reek wouldn't see me.

Right inside the door, the big man had a chicken on a balance scale. He used more care weighing the chicken than a jeweler would weighing a stone.

I sidled up close to Ceece. "Why's he taking so much pains weighing them chickens?"

"Why, he weighs'em, then matches the chickens up so's the ones fighting will pert-near weigh the same. A quarter-ounce is all the differ--" Ceece's eye caught an almost-pure-white rooster, and he was gone.

Buying myself another biscuit, I threw the fatback at a dog beside the wall. It was hard to figure why they put so much stock in these chickens.

I stood way back in the corner and tried to keep out of sight. I sure didn't want Reek to see me. Ceece stood right in the middle, big as you please. By the way he acted, I didn't see how he intended to steal chickens. I knew Ceece--he was up to some tom-foolery.

All at once folks started to crowd into the barn. In a few minutes, all the seats filled up. There was lots of low talking and laughter.

Two men stood facing each other across the pit. Each held a rooster under his arm. The pit boss stepped in between them and crossed his arms over his chest like an army general.

When the pit boss made a funny motion with his hands, the two men kneeled down in the pit. Each put his chicken between the palms of his hands. The pit boss nodded his head and each man set his chicken down on the dirt. At the same time the two men reached into their hip pockets and brought out shinny pieces of metal about five inches long. They looked like little spears. Even in the dim light of the barn, they sparkled. The two men used leather straps to fasten the metal pieces on the chickens' legs where their spurs grew.

Ceece came up about that time. "What's them things?" I said. Why are the men holding the chickens?

"Why, them there is gaffs. Sharp as locust thorns. Boy, them are the handlers, they tend the chickens during the fight."

Not knowing enough about chicken fighting to ask questions, I kneeled down beside the wall to watch. The handlers and the chickens stared at each other like they were blood enemies.

"For sure, that red rooster is a fighter," an old man said from behind me. "I seed his daddy fight many a time."

"Well," another farmer said. "I'll wager a dollar on t'other."

Betting went on all over the place for ten or so minutes. Most bets were less than a dollar. Two men started talking about a five-dollar bet. The place grew quiet when everybody stopped and listened.

"Which one do you like?" Mr. Seth Vest said, waving a ten-dollar bill in Simon Boggwater's face. Seth went around the room waving the bill in folks' face, and asking which chicken they would bet on. I knew that most of the men didn't have that kind of money. When he asked Will Gorman which chicken he liked, Will reached for the wallet in his overall pocket. "I like the brown and red."

Seth stepped back. "Eh, eh. Me too, I guess we cain't bet." In a flash Seth was over near where I was.

Will Gorman turned and went right on talking to some farmers, as if he knew what Seth would do.

"Seth, he does that all the time," a man said. "He ain't made a wager, to my knowledge, since they built the first barn back in the twenties."

I saw Perd Driddle come in the other side of the barn. Perd was a little wisp of a man whose spectacles sat on the end of his nose. He sat down on the front row about ten feet from me.

It was a known fact that Seth Vest harbored a grudge against him. Perd had come home from the first big war and married the girl Seth had been courting. "Seth was gathering twigs and making a

162

nest when Perd ran off with his hen," Dad had said, when Seth and Perd were talked about at the house.

Seth stared at Perd and reached in his bib pocket so fast I thought for sure he was about to pull a gun. Even though I was a good ways from him it scared me.

In place of a gun, Seth jerked out a money clip, ruffled through it, and yanked out a fifty-dollar bill. I had never seen one. It looked as big as a bed sheet. He waved it in the direction of Perd. I could tell he wanted to go over and mock Perd with the bill, but the place was so crowded he couldn't make his way over.

When the two men finished fastening the steel to their chickens' legs, they backed up and stood against the little wall of the pit. All at once, the pit boss dropped his arms to his sides. The two men walked to the center of the pit, holding the chickens out like they intended to swap them. The men stared at each other like they were fixing to fight. An hour earlier, I had seen them leaning on the back of a wagon talking like old friends. They rubbed the chicken's beaks together. Each rooster commenced pecking at the other.

The pit boss raised his arms and gave another signal. "Pit'em!"

The two men dropped their chickens to the ground. Both roosters commenced fighting like you have never seen. Flying into each other, they hit so

163

hard they both fell backwards. They jumped up and went right back at it, each one trying to climb up the other's chest. That went on for maybe three minutes. Neither chicken seemed to be tiring. All at once, the red rooster got his steel gaff hung in the side of the other. Neither one could get to their feet.

The men were at the chickens' sides in a flash, with the pit boss standing over them. The men picked up their chickens like they were holding babies. They were held together by the gaff. The men worked slow, under the eye of the pit boss.

"The man who owns the chicken with the gaff stuck in it pulls them apart," Ceece said, low in my ear.

"That's the reason they are so careful," I said.

"Yeah, otherwise that man who owns the chicken with the gaff stuck could twist it and kill the other fellow's bird. Boy! you don't know nothin?"

"He wouldn't do that."

Ceece stared at me like I had lost my mind. "Boy, there's money changing hands, boy. Folks do peculiar thangs where money talks. That's why the pit boss is so strict."

"Don't call me boy," I said. "I don't care for this whole business of chicken fighting."

The man whose chicken had got stuck studied the wound. Blood gushed out all over his hands. He pushed his thumb against the chicken's neck real hard--the blood slowed to a trickle in no time flat. I wanted to ask Ceece how the man had stopped the blood, but I was too mad at him.

The pit boss looked at his watch. Seconds later he gave the signal and the fight started again. Both birds flew at each other over and over again. They stopped twice for the gaffs to be pulled out, once from each bird.

All at once, the red chicken staggered like it was drunk. It kept trying to fight, but its head drooped lower and lower. The other rooster jumped on him and cut with every flutter. The wounded bird was dead by the time the pit boss signaled. Both handlers went to the center and picked up their birds.

Money changed hands all through the crowd. Ceece looked at the dead chicken when the man walked by. "Shit. Dead as a doornail."

"I can see that," I said. "That salty pork is making me crave water." I made my way out of the barn, and headed for the spring. I wasn't real thirsty. I wanted to get away from Ceece and the chicken fight.

Chicken fighting didn't have a hold on me like it did on Ceece, but a while later I went back to the barn anyway. Outside the back door, in the dirt, laid three dead chickens. The smell was not bad enough to cause me to be sick, but it had drawn bugs. Flies swarmed all around the place.

When I made my way back into the barn, I
found a seat down against the bottom row. The
chickens doing the fighting in the pit looked enough
alike to be twins. They must have been at it for a
long time, judging from the way they staggered.
Each bird had worked hard, yet they didn't seem to
have much blood leaking anywhere. It seemed like
the chickens didn't have enough strength left to cut
each other. They flew into one another, but neither
rose over a few inches from the ground. The gaffs
never left the dirt. A few minutes later they laid
almost a foot apart, pecking at the air. Both of the
handlers looked tuckered out, too.

"Damn," Ceece said over my shoulder. "Them
is two fine chickens. I wish there was a way to get
our hands on'em, but their owners will want'em to
fight again."

"Draw," the pit boss said, signaling with his
palms down.

The handlers picked up the birds and walked
out the front door. Two other men came into the pit
holding chickens under their arms.

About a dozen men gathered up in the seats
beside where I sat. They talked in low voices.

"I'll go seven dollars," Mr. Joe Harvie said.

It was a lot of money for Mr. Harvie. I had
courted one of his daughters for a spell. He was
known all over the valley as a miser.

Another man reached into his bib pocket and
pulled out a wadded-up bill. "Here's a ten-er."

Down from me, a man passed a wad of one-dollar bills to me. I hunkered down so Mr. Harvie wouldn't recognize me. He paid no mind as I passed the money to the man beside me.

Mr. Harvie waved at Perd, who came slipping down across the seats. Perd walked around like he was walking on eggs. His face showed signs of being afraid, and he had the look of a whipped pup at the same time.

A man handed some money to Perd. "Here's twenty-seven."

Perd went tiptoeing back around the pit and climbed into his seat.

"What in the world are they up to?" I said to Ceece.

He rubbed his elbow against my ribs and muttered about the chickens like he had money to bet.

I saw other men hand Perd money. Surely, he wasn't taking on all these bets. Besides, he wasn't keeping up with where the money came from.

Down in the pit, two different men showed off their roosters. One was brown and red colored. The other looked like the one Ceece had called a Roundhead.

Seth Vest waved his fifty-dollar bill in front of the crowd. He strutted around the pit one whole turn. I could tell he was having the time of his life. He sure would rub it in if he could. Seth spied Perd and bounded across the seats, stepping on some people's hands. Seth waved the bill right under Perd's nose. "Which bird do you like, for this fifty?"

Perd's face turned red. "I like the little brown-and-red."

"Me--ug--to," Seth said, trying to keep his balance. He almost fell backwards and stepped on a man's hand.

The man stood up--he had to be near seven feet tall. He shoved Seth back toward Perd. "Watch what in the hell you're a'doin."

Perd grinned. "Well, in that case I'll take the Roundhead."

It was so quiet in the barn I could almost hear the chickens breathing. Seth's Adam's apple jumped up and down. He looked all around the barn; every eye was on him. Sweat popped out on his forehead.

The big pit boss came up behind Seth. "I'll hold the money."

Quick as a wink, Perd handed the big man the wadded up bills. Seth looked like an egg-sucking dog as he handed the big man the fifty-dollar bill.

"You've got yourself a wager." The tone of the pit boss' voice made it known to Seth that there would be no weaseling out.

There was not one other bet made. I kneeled down close to the pit and even forgot that Reek or somebody might tell my folks about me being there.

Everybody in the barn pulled for Perd's rooster. The fight started; Seth's rooster flogged Perd's good the first two times they flew into each other. A knot came up in my stomach. I felt sure that Perd's rooster was a goner, until a man put his hand on my shoulder. "Shaw, don't fret, that Roundhead is a good'un." I knew Reek's voice, but he never let on that he was talking to me.

On and on the chickens fought. Perd's rooster got stuck with a gaff. A loud "Ah! Ah!" filled the barn when we saw the chicken dragging its left wing. I looked over my shoulder. Reek's eyes were fixed on the pit.

My nerves twitched like I had money riding on the fight. It was all I could do to keep from jumping up and heading for the door.

I looked at Seth. The color had come back in his face. On the other hand, Perd's face was as long as a pitchfork handle.

I wanted the pit boss to stop the fight long enough for the handler to see what he could do to help Perd's wounded rooster. In place of that, he just crossed his arms and watched. All at once Perd's rooster circled to its left, keeping the bad wing toward the other bird.

Seth's bird stood in the center like it didn't know what was taking place. I hoped this would give Perd's rooster long enough to get some strength back. Seth's chicken flew on top of Perd's rooster and knocked it against the pit wall. Seth's bird sank a gaff--pinned Perd's rooster against the ground where it couldn't fight back. I couldn't see any way the bird could stay alive long.

"That pit boss is taking his sweet time stopping this thing!" It came out before I thought.

Reek's big hand squeezed my shoulder again. I didn't look back, and he didn't say anything.

The pit boss signaled, and the two men picked up their birds. Was he going to declare Seth's bird the winner? I hated for that to happen, but I wanted the thing to be over, no matter how much it hurt.

"Perd's blamed old rooster looks bad a sight," Ceece said.

"Damn, I can see that," I said. "As luck would have it the poor thing will take forever getting itself killed."

Seth pranced around. He could already feel the hundred dollars in his grubby hands. Chicken fighting was something I could do without.

The pit boss dropped his arms. "Pit'em!"

Seth's chicken pounced on Perd's the first time they circled--had the rooster pinned down in fifteen seconds--Seth's chicken pecked hard enough to draw blood from Perd's rooster's head.

I didn't want to watch Seth take all the men's money from the pit boss. I stood up to leave, but there was no way to get through the crowd.

Seth's bird got its gaff stuck in Perd's rooster and the pit boss stopped the fight another time. The handlers pulled the birds apart. With the bad wing,

Perd's rooster couldn't keep from getting cut to pieces. It had no place to run and couldn't fly. Before long, Seth's bird was going to stick the gaff into the right place and make a kill.

In no time flat, Perd's rooster was pinned against the ground and the pit wall. Every time it moved it left a red spot in the dirt.

"It's the same thing; it happens every time," I said under my breath when the pit boss stopped the fight. The handlers pulled the chickens apart and held the birds' noses together. Seth's bird pecked at Perd's--it didn't peck back. Blood went drip-drip-drip-drip from what was left of Perd's rooster.

Everyone stood staring at the pit. I wondered if they wanted it to be over as much as I did.

Maybe there was no way to stop the bird's wing from bleeding now. Its handler didn't even try. I looked toward the door. No way was I going to stay and see Seth strut around with the men's money.

Before I could make my way out, the pit boss signaled for them to start fighting again. Perd's rooster circled slower now. Seth's bird moved in for the kill. It flew a foot high--I saw that it would land square on top of Perd's rooster. The gaffs shined like new ice picks as they came down toward the back of Perd's rooster.

Like a dart, Perd's rooster spun to its left. This time Seth's chicken landed against the rail. Perd's rooster was on top in a flash. It grabbed Seth's chicken by its comb. Seth's chicken tried every way in the world to shake it loose. They circled the pit twice--Perd's rooster held on like glue on cotton.

"Land sakes alive, he's a'holdin on like a bulldog!" a voice up in the seats said.

The gaffs flew like flashes of light--Perd's rooster cut with every swipe--Seth's chicken dug into the ground.

"Call time!" Seth said. "They're hung up!"

The pit boss gave him the eagle eye. Perd's rooster didn't stab--it cut. Not one time did its gaffs hang. Seth's chicken got weak as its blood drained out. In less than a minute it couldn't raise its head. Perd's rooster walked right up on the other's back.

In place of signaling, the pit boss walked into the pit. "Fight's over."

"Shaw, shaw." Reek put his hand on my arm. "Seth's face is so long, hit'll take three packs of razor blades to shave him."

I looked, but all I saw was Seth's back going through the door.

When I turned around, Reek was trying to drum up a knife swap with a man from town.

Ceece ran over to me. "Come on." We went out the back door. He bent down over the dead chickens and commenced throwing them into two piles.

"What are you doing?" I said.

"Sorting them out. Gonna save some of'em." He looked one rooster over, stuck its head in his mouth, and sucked out a wad of dried blood and stuff. It was hard for me not to puke on the dead chickens.

Ceece spat out a mouthful. "These here got some life left in them." He ran up the spring branch with a chicken under each arm.

"You want this moss-trooper?" a man held out Perd's rooster.

"I sure do," I said before I thought.

When I got to the spring, Ceece had one chicken buried in some black moss so only its head stuck out. Ceece jerked the feathers out of another one's side like he intended to pluck it alive. He pulled a rusty needle and spool of thread from the shoebox. He shut the lid fast.

"Don't you burn the needle, like Mama does before she sews a body's skin?" I said.

"Boy, this here's a chicken," Ceece said, pulling the thread through the needle with his bloody teeth.

I watched while Ceece worked for well over an hour. A time or two, I felt he was going to kill the thing for sure. He cut its belly open with his pocketknife and washed out its insides. After he had the chicken sewed up, he stuck its head under a wing and fouled it with a stick. I stood and watched. We had put chickens to sleep many a time that way, but I saw no reason to do it here.

Laying the bird down carefully he pulled the other out of the moss. While he held it out in front

173

of his chest, he turned to me. "By golly, the least you could do is wash the blood off your chicken."

I started to tell him to go jump. It didn't set well, him bossing me around, but he did seem to know more than I did about doctoring chickens. For well over an hour, I washed my chicken.

My chicken didn't have anything wrong with it except the wing. It had been clipped, like a body does to keep one from flying over a fence. It would never fly again, but I couldn't find anything else wrong.

"What are we going to do with all these roosters?" I said. "'Less you know some trick, we cain't raise no biddies from a flock of roosters."

"We'll get us a pullet from one of the wagons out front."

"I know for a fact you don't have any money-- told you we'd not be stealin chickens."

He grinned real big. "What about eggs?"

"Well, well, well. I hadn't thought of that."

Ceece grabbed up all the chickens and the shoebox and headed for the barn. "Hurry, they'll be breaking up a'fore long."

We ran down to where the wagons were. Ceece opened the shoebox and pulled newspaper from around five small eggs. I followed him among the wagons until he stopped at a green one with chickens in the bed.

Ceece looked around like he was trying to hide himself from the barn. As pretty as you please, he climbed up in the wagon.

I stepped on the wagon hub and looked over the side. He lifted up a hen and looked at her eggs. The hen didn't squawk. She was most likely scared as much as me.

"What in the world . . ." I said.

"Watch that blamed barn, will you," He said, carefully slipping the eggs from under a game hen. "I don't want to be caught switching these." He placed the eggs from his box under the hen.

"I told you before we came, I don't want no part of chicken stealing."

"An egg--hell fire--ain't no blamed chicken. This old sister will never know the difference, a hundred years from now."

"Ceece," I said.

"Watch the darn barn," he switched eggs with two more hens.

"Ceece," I said.

He jumped down from the third wagon, holding the game chicken eggs in both hands. I thought about grabbing them and breaking them over the rocks sticking up everywhere in the field. He took off running back toward the spring with the shoebox under his arm and both hands full of eggs.

"Why don't you set these eggs for me?" Ceece said, when we were half way up the cove road.

175

"Foxes will find and suck them. They get half of Mama's."

"Why don't you hatch 'em out around your cook stove?"

"Hell no. I ain't wet-nursin no eggs you stole. Mama would have me beat to death before the three weeks it takes for them to hatch."

His face dropped. "I ain't got no hen to set them under."

I crossed the foot log before I spoke. "Well, I'll give you a hen. There's one fixing to set in that pile of slabs between the hog lot and corncrib. You might as well steal her too."

Mama met me at the kitchen door. She gave the rooster and me a look that would melt iron. "Where'd you get that?"

I had trouble getting my tongue to work. "He ain't much, but he--he crows good."

"You stole him, I'd bet. I'll tend to you if that's a fact."

I held the rooster out in front of her. His bad wing drooped down like a wash rag. "No, honest, A man gave him to me. See this bad wing?"

She eyed the hedge bush, the one where she cut limbs when she figured on giving one of us a thrashing. Mama was not a big woman, but she sure got mad as the devil sometimes.

I set the rooster up on a rail Dad had laid on the garden fence to hold up his grapevines. The rooster reared back and crowed twice. Why couldn't he keep his mouth shut? I felt like wringing his neck.

Mama's heart softened, like it did where critters were concerned. "Just like all men, crows to himself even when there ain't no women folks to listen."

"I gotta go help Dad and Reek with feeding." Backing up a few steps, I turned and beat it down to the barn before she had a chance to ask anything else.

Anybody could see that the rooster wouldn't ever be able to fly again. I nailed some pieces of wood on a pole so he had a way to climb up to roost in a hemlock down by the branch.

Two days later Dad and Reek wanted to go fishing. They fished in spells. When they fished, it was everything in the world they wanted to do. In the next few weeks, we spent almost all the time tramping a riverbank. I was glad to go. Keeping that bigmouth Ceece away from our house would let time pass so Mama would get used to having the rooster around.

The Friday evening before the first frost, Reek spat snuff on a worm he was putting on a hook. "Shaw, for a fact, thar's a rain a'comin. A real frog-strangler."

The next morning it was raining like pouring water out of a bucket. We had fished out. Even

Dad and Reek owned up to the fact that they'd had enough. Of course, this wouldn't last past the first two pretty days. I had finished eating and hoped to sleep some before my little sisters got up.

Ceece made more racket than the rain falling on the tin roof when he came up on the porch. "Wake up," he said. "We've got to go to the chicken fight. It's the last one this year."

"Shut your fool mouth. Mama'll get word about that barn and I'll catch the devil."

"I saw her and your Dad leave as I come up on the porch."

"Cain't you see the rain? Have you eat all the chickens and eggs you stole?"

Mama and Dad spent some of their Saturday mornings by themselves up in the bee house or else they went loafering off somewhere.

It took Ceece an hour to talk me into going. I wouldn't have gone at all if he had not bellowed at the top of his lungs. Anyhow, them nosy sisters would remember everything we said, even though they hadn't moved since Ceece came in.

"It's bound to break off this raining soon," Ceece said.

Nothing would do him but for me to go, or whack him good. Then, he'd go pout a while and I'd feel bad. The sisters stirred; they would tell on me either way. I looked out the window and could see a patch of clear sky about the size of a man's hand.

Pulling my boots on, I looked Ceece in the eye. "You steal one thing and I'll wait on you. Besides, keep you tongue in your mouth until were gone."

Ceece picked up a paper box he'd left on the porch. It was twice the size of the shoebox he'd carried before. This one had holes cut in the sides. I muttered, "I'll throw that thing in the creek the first time you try to steal anything."

Both of us were bareheaded and were wet to our waists before the rain stopped. Ceece talked a mile a minute. He held the paper box under his shirt like it was filled with sugar. When we reached the bridge over Junaluska Creek I finally got word in edge-ways. "Did the eggs you stole hatch?"

"Hell, no! Nary a one of that batch. I'll take that back, one did but it died that very night."

"What do you mean, it died? Why didn't you look after it better?"

"Drowned, it did. Fell in the creek, or at least that's where I found it the next morning."

"You don't seem too put out about it. By the way, how many eggs you stole since then?"

"A few. I'll have enough gamecocks shortly to take'em all on. I even got two hens last time."

"How long will it be before you, eh, we get caught? Taking a wounded rooster is one thing, stealing hens and eggs is another. I'm a good mind to turn around right now."

"Hell fire, I'm too keen for'em to catch me. I'll be a big-time chicken man shortly."

No sooner had we started walking through where the wagons were parked than I felt a big hand on my left shoulder. Another hand landed on my right arm.

Ceece's eyes bulged out as two big hands yoked him around his neck. Ceece wiggled like a worm in hot ashes. "What do-do-do you want?" he blurted out.

I saw right off that the man who had Ceece was the one who owned the wagon where Ceece had switched the eggs. Faster than a body can say scat, there were at least a dozen men standing behind us. We were in trouble and I didn't know how much. With Ceece being the way he was, most likely it was a heap.

The man's hand on my shoulder tightened. "You're the very ones that switched eggs."

I didn't say a word, but Ceece's tongue wagged like a bell clapper. "Why, why, I never switched no eggs. It weren't me. What you claim I did it for? Let a'loose of me!"

By now, the people gathered around were five deep. I felt a little better when I looked for Reek or anybody from over the cove way and didn't see a soul I knew. I worried more about what Dad would do to me than what the men were planning on.

Ceece tried to jerk free. The man's grip on my shoulder tightened. Ceece's feet come blame-near off the ground. I didn't struggle--it was plain the men meant to do what they pleased with us. If they'd have let me, I'd have beat the tar out of that Ceece, right then.

The man tightened his grip more. "You kill somebody, boy, and folks forget it in five years. You get caught stealing, and twenty years later, when somebody asks, 'What does he do?' the other will answer, 'Don't know but he used to be a thief.'"

I tried my best to keep my shoulder from shaking by tightening up my whole body. The hand felt like a vice.

"Clem." A voice came from back in the crowd. "What are you a'fixin to do with them, now that you've caught'em?"

My shoulder shook in spite of all I could do. I'd heard of the Rankins many times. They lived way back on Sweat Heffer Creek. Clem had the name of being one of the meanest men that ever come from these parts. He farmed the rockiest mountainsides anywhere about. If people stopped in the road below where Clem was in his fields, he threw rocks at them.

"I'd say them eggs was worth four dollars. I'm a good mind to take it out of their hides."

"Them eggs was our'n," Ceece blurted out.

Someone threw a big pile of leather at our feet. "Use these check lines on'em."

It didn't matter much what he did to me--Mama would have Dad do worse when they heard about it. Ceece stared at the pile of leather. I started to tell them that I had no ownership in any chickens. My chin quivered so bad I couldn't talk.

"Clem." It was the voice from the crowd. "Don't your corn need gathering and your taters dug?"

I saw the color come back in Ceece's face when the big hands loosened their grip. I knew what Ceece was about to do. If they turned him loose, he'd hit the timber.

"Be at my house at six o'clock Saturday morning," Clem said. "I'll let you boys work off the eggs you thieved."

"Yeah! Yeah!" Ceece said.

If Ceece ever got out of the man's grip, he'd be short off and long gone. The thought had crossed my mind too. I would sure give up my going to the chicken fights if it would get me out of this mess.

"Remember," Clem said, "I know who you are, Quill Vance, and I know where Rail Cove is."

We didn't let any moss grow under our feet as we beat it for home. Half way up the cove I put my hand on Ceece's arm. "You will come down early enough Saturday so's we can gather the corn and get the taters out in one day."

182

"Shore."

I knew Ceece had no idea of going with me. He could think up a hundred ways to keep from it. Even right then he coughed and wiped his hand across his nose, like he was coming down with a cold. At first, I got a little tickled at him.

"Well, I don't see no way anybody can make me gather corn for nothin. We can dodge aroun--"

I flew mad. "Ceece, this time if'en you don't help me, I'll flatten that banana nose all over your face."

"Oh! I'll be right thar."

With my right hand, I tapped him on the nose. Then I crossed the foot log to the house.

Once on the next Thursday and twice on Friday, Ceece came down and tried to weasel out. Both times I tapped him on the nose and he shut up.

Ceece wasn't more'en fifteen minutes late Saturday morning. He coughed once when he came through the kitchen door. Then he forgot all about being sick; he dug into the table full of food Mama had set out. Her and Dad had already gathered up my sisters and left, so I didn't have to worry about Ceece running his mouth.

While he sopped up a wad of gravy and eggs with a biscuit, Ceece allowed, "I've got to get back early. I'll help you til morning is over."

I reached over, grabbed his left ear, and twisted it hard. I led him out the door, still twisting. "Big boy, you better do some steppin and fetchin then."

We made it to the Rankins place while the first rays of sun glistened on the dew. Their house sat three hundred yards up on a hillside, with corn on all sides. Off near the woods was a gully that held a pole shed. The land was so steep the porch must have been thirty feet high. I climbed the narrow steps ahead of Ceece.

Clem walked to the edge of the porch and pointed toward the shed. "The mule is in the barn and the sled is up yonder by the spring." He turned and went back into the house.

"Ain't he gonna help us?" Ceece said, when I almost stepped on his hand going down the steps.

We walked to the shed that Clem had called a barn. Ceece ranted. "By rights, them eggs ain't worth no four dollars. Hell fire, we got to gather this corn and it ain't knee-high to a duck."

"Shut up."

A little gray mule stood in the shed facing the door. It was so poor I could stand in front of it and count its ribs. The mule didn't flinch as I slipped the bridle over its head.

Ceece walked around like he was lost. I pointed to the collar hanging on a post. "Ain't you going to help?"

"That--that thar is a white mule; they mean."

"Hell fire, Ceece he ain't no bigger than you."

Ceece tried to put the gears on the mule without getting close to either end. "Boo," I said, causing him to run into the wall.

A few minutes later he got a corn stalk and tried to use it to fasten the trace chains. It made him a bit mad when I laughed in his face. "You hold his head and I'll hook him up."

"Let's dig the taters first," Ceece said.

I gave him a dirty look and clucked to the mule. The little mule pulled the sled over the steep, rocky ground as good as a body could ask for. He weaved in and out of the big boulders like he remembered where each one was.

The ears of corn were not much size, so we covered a lot of ground before the sled was full. Like always, Ceece thought and thought of some way to beat his way through. "Clem won't climb up this sidling ground to see if we gathered these last few rows."

"The hell you say. He'll watch us like a hawk. After all, you're a thief."

We jerked the corn off the stalks and threw it in the sled fast, and by midmorning all the corn above the house was in the shed. Me working on one side of the sled and Ceece on the other, we couldn't talk much. That suited me.

When we got near the house, a girl came down the steps with a clay jug in one hand and a gourd in the other. She had auburn hair and eyes big as a calf's. My heart pounded like a hammer mill. The thin flour-sack dress fit her body like a worn glove. She smiled when I took the gourd and spilled water down my chin, wetting the whole front of my shirt.

"I don't want none of you'ens water." Ceece said. when she tried to hand him the gourd.

Like a flash, she was gone. We watched until she climbed the last step onto the porch. I sputtered out "Wait, what's your name?"

"Why, she ain't pretty. Her waist ain't no bigger than a wasp's."

"Damn, Ceece she's a fine looking thing. I think I'm in love. She's prettier than the pictures of them girls in the woman's underwear catalog you're always trying to show me. Yes-sir-ee, I'm in love."

"Didn't you see how dirty her right knee is?"

"Hell fire, that's the prettiest set of legs I ever seen. Are you blind?"

"Huuugh."

I jerked an ear of corn from a stalk and threw it hard as I could. It hit Ceece on the left shoulder. "Damn you, don't you say a word or start bawling."

By the time the sun was a quarter-down, the corn was in the shed. "Here, little fellow," I said, throwing twelve ears of corn in the mule's feed box. "This is the best feeding you've had in a spell."

"You'll founder that little mule," Ceece said.

Ceece looked at me funny when I said, "Mules ain't like any horse. A horse will eat til his gut busts, but a mule will eat enough to do him and leave the rest for later."

We found a potato digger hanging on the garden fence and two rusty buckets with toe sacks stuffed in the bottom to stop up the holes. It was not long before we both broke a sweat digging in the rocky ground.

Ceece started quarreling. "No wonder Clem didn't grabble these taters before now. He was waiting for a couple of suckers like us to come along."

None of the potatoes were any size. I tried not to think about anything. This was a lot harder than pulling corn. Sparks flew with every lick when the tines hit the flint rocks.

Ceece mumbled, "I'm about to drop in my tracks."

Clem came down toward the patch with what had to be their water bucket in his hand. He stood on the hill above us with his arms crossed. "Hole up these spuds in the bank behind the house. Mind you--don't skin'em up. I mean to save every one of'em. Little'uns make good hog feed."

Ceece's face was as red as a pickled beet. He kicked at the ground. "Ain't none of these taters big as a glass marble. We ought'a throw these buckets in the creek; we've done and worked out four eggs, even if'en they was gold."

My second wind had come and I felt better. "You'll sleep good tonight," I said.

"Where's that skinny girl with the water jug?" Ceece said. "I'll go dig a ditch to hole these taters in."

By the time I got all the potatoes out of the ground, a good breeze had commenced to blow. I didn't even think about what Mama and Dad might do to me. I thought about the girl. We hadn't seen her since way earlier.

Fifty feet above the house, Ceece found a broken-handle shovel and started digging a ditch. Dirt flew like a hundred ground hogs were at it. "Ceece, don't throw that dirt down hill, we'll need it to cover these potatoes back up with."

"Oh, hell fire, I'm digging this ditch."

Once the potatoes were laid in the ditch, we covered them with straw and dry weeds. I sat down on the steps and pointed my finger at Ceece. "You fill the ditch with the dirt you piled down the hill, and I'll do the fine covering."

I watched Ceece while he sweated. Taking my bandana out, I wiped my head until it was sore, hoping it would cause the girl to bring more water. She never showed her face. That made me madder at Ceece than anything.

Ceece was more afraid of the dark than of a bear, so I go. "You'd better get a hurry on--it'll be dark in a little bit."

It felt good when the mound of dirt looked like it would shed water. We went to the spring and drank like camels.

We finished drinking and I sat down on a rock where I could see if the girl came out of the house. I felt a cool breeze blowing up the hillside.

Ceece stood close to the spring. He started to unbutton the fly on his britches.

"You piss in that spring," I said, "and I'll rock you all the way home."

Ceece backed up two steps, and buttoned his britches back up. He looked at me for a long time like I'd stole his candy. He backed up two more steps, spit in the spring, and lit out toward home.

THE DRUMMER -- Come-a-Calling

We hadn't been in the feed store five minutes when he tore through the door, bouncing along like a little kid going to get candy.

"Morning all, Elmer C Spinsworthy come-a-calling," he said, dropping the big leather satchel. It shook the floor like he'd dropped an anvil.

"Morning, Spinsworthy," the feed store man said, without looking up.

"Would you believe . . . I came upon a store down on the Angle Fork of the Pigeon River a while back; every shelf in the place was lined with matches. Boxes on top of boxes were stacked to the ceiling. Never seen so many matches in my born days."

The short, bald man pranced around and pointed with his little derby hat at the shelves. I thought once he was going to jump over the counter. His Adam's apple bounced up and down inside the button-down collar, which didn't match the shirt at all. The collar was snow white; the shirt was dingy brown. He put me in mind of a little bantam rooster.

"Maybe he sold a lot of matches," the feed store man said.

"Would you believe that's exactly what I said to him? 'You must sell a whale of a lot of matches.'"

"What did he say to that?" the feed store man said.

Spinsworthy slapped his fat thigh with his hat. "He say's to me, 'No, I hardly sell any, but thar's a man comes through here once a month that can sure to hell sell'em.'"

The feed store man turned red as a beet. "Elmer you're the only man in the world windy enough to blow up a fish net like a balloon."

"I'll take a dying oath," Spinsworthy said. "Or, or something like that."

I had heard of this Elmer Spinsworthy fellow all my life, but this was my first time to come face to face with him.

I remembered what Mama said a week ago Friday when she caught my older sisters running their mouths about some people they didn't know. "'There ain't a stranger in this whole wide country. I've traveled all over, and if there is, I ain't never met up with him.' Them's the words of Elmer C Spinsworthy, a well liked man. You-all take that to heart. Quit gabbing about people you've not met."

Spinsworthy wasn't a bit over five feet tall, and his suspenders stretched like banjo strings over the roll of fat around his middle. The thing that stood out the most about him was his head. It seemed way to little for the rest of his body. All in all, I could see why I had heard his name spoke so many times. He sure was somebody you couldn't forget easy.

"He's the last drummer left in these parts," Dad said while we were in the back standing by a stack of hog feed.

"What's a drummer?" I said.

"There used to be plenty of them coming through these mountains. They carried their goods with them and went from house to house. Why, even a hotel down in the county seat was called the Drummer's House."

"What happened to them?"

"They're called salesmen now-a-days. Don't stop nowhere except at stores. They take orders for goods, which get brought by trucks. Put many a drummer out of business--all but Spinsworthy."

"How does this Spinsworthy work?" I said.

"He comes here on the train ever month or so, rents a hack and travels the back ways, selling his wares."

"I see," I said.

Dad walked out toward the truck. He put his foot up on the running board and turned to me. "I'm going on into town," he said. "Want'a come along?"

"No, I think I'll hang around here for a spell. Maybe I'll just walk on to town later."

Dad drove off. I knew he was headed to the poolroom. I didn't like to go there much. How they could sit for hours and watch someone knock little balls around was beyond me. Besides, if he ran into Reek Moore they'd take off somewhere to swap coon dogs.

"Let me show you the latest thing from Chicago." Spinsworthy's voice came from inside the feed store. By the time I got through the door, he was lifting the big leather bag up on the counter, with both hands. Out fell everything from a cooking pot to a thimble. I didn't know if the stuff was any good or not, but I could tell right off the pocket knives were the cheap, shiny kind. I'd had one once, and it wouldn't hold an edge, no matter how often you whetted it.

The feed store man leaned over the counter in Spinsworthy's face. "Got any matches?"

I laughed under my breath.

"Got enough to burn a wet dog," Spinsworthy said, spitting on a little hand mirror and wiping it off with his sleeve.

When it was all said and done, the feed store man had bought a few things, but not nigh as much as Spinsworthy had wanted him too.

"You cain't buy good mercantile from them Johnny-come-lately salesmen," Spinsworthy said. "Never see what you're getting until it's too late."

"I'll make out," the feed store man said.

"You old skinflint. Would you believe . . . I need a body to drive this hack back when I get over to Eastfelt. There, I catch the evening train."

"How so?" The feed store man said.

"Would you believe? They will charge me two dollars if I leave it over there."

"Bring it back here and catch the train."

"No way, I'm a traveling man. Got stops to make, where the folks ain't so stingy." Spinsworthy looked straight toward me. There wasn't anyone else in the store.

"How much you pay?" The feed store man said.

"Fifty cents."

"Dollar." The feed store man said.

"Would you believe the prices these days? I'll give sixty cents."

My face turned red; I felt heat on the back of my neck. I hadn't come here looking for a job, yet the thought of driving a hack did set well. I'd have drove the thing for nothing if he'd asked. All I'd ever drove was a mule and sled. That sure wasn't no fun. You couldn't stay in the sled over the rocky ground we owned. Skidding pole wood off the ridges was hard work. This way I'd get to ride on a spring seat.

"Seventy-five cents. Top pay."

"Go with him son," the feed store man said, "if you want. You'll learn how to lie."

I followed Spinsworthy around to the side of the building to where the wagon sat. The sorrel mare stood with one foot propped up on a rock, sound asleep.

"Keep a good eye about you," Spinsworthy said, heaving the big leather bag onto the wagon. "I've got a load of good and valuable mercantile."

I didn't answer. The old stable mare knew a right smart more than I did when it came to pulling a wagon. By that time, the sun was hitting down in the valley and it didn't take much prodding to get the mare started.

It wasn't far over to Eastfelt. Taking the river road, we could make it in something over an hour in the truck. I looked up at the high peaks all around. Going over the mountain was closer. I'd be back while the sun was still high on Forney Bald.

The mare walked slow and steady. She picked where she stepped to make it easier on her feet.

"Con-found that horse." Spinsworthy said, when the wagon wheel would hit a rock, causing his stuff in the bed to rattle.

The crunch, crunch of the steel wheels crushing the small rocks made me glad I'd come. Looking back at the straight silver streaks in the wet road, I felt like a big-time teamster.

We hadn't gone more'en a mile when he pointed to a road leading up the side of a steep ridge. I had been up the road before on foot. About everybody knew the place as the Bluff. There was at least a dozen switchbacks, before the road topped out.

But what bothered me the most was a big rock that reached all the way across the road for a hundred feet or better. Not only that, it leaned down to the right so steep that a body couldn't stand up on it. Right below the rock was a bluff that dropped off two hundred feet into the river. Folks had walked around the thing for so long they'd cut a foot-wide trail on the upper side.

"A half a mile up ahead the road is one big slick rock," I said. "Steep as the mare's face."

"Let me drive," Spinsworthy said swinging his short, stubby leg over the back of the seat.

"A body can barely stand up on that rock. I'll walk and lead the horse."

"I'll have you know that I happen to be a master teamster," Spinsworthy said, once he settled in the seat on my left.

By the time we'd reached the third switchback, the road had got steeper and narrower. The old mare stopped and got her breath. I could see the big rock. At first, a body would think it was a patch of gray pipe clay. I knew it was wet gray granite, polished by time and weather until it was as slick as a turning plow point. From the wagon seat, it looked scarier than it had on foot.

Since I'd been on this road, someone had laid a breastwork of locust poles against the trees along the lower side. If we drove the wagon down where the wheels would run against the logs, and the mare didn't stumble we might make it.

Spinsworthy clucked to the horse and we headed for the rock. "Gitty-up, gitty-up!"

"You need to stay down against the breast-works, on the lower side of the rock," I said

"Would you believe . . . it's potter's clay."

Spinsworthy pulled the left rein and the mare started toward the high side of the rock.

"I'll lead her," I said "drive down next to the breastwork--"

Before I got the words out the mare was well out on the rock. She was pulling for all she was worth.

All at once, the wagon skidded to the right. It slid slow at first, but before I could raise up out of the seat it slid like the rock had been greased with butter.

The wagon was well below the horse. She stumbled to her knees. Once the trace chains were slack, the wagon slid faster and faster. Spinsworthy tried to climb out over the upper side of the wagon, but it was leaning to the right so bad he fell on top of me. His weight knocked me back against the lower side. He ended up on top of me in the floorboard. I couldn't get my breath with all that blubber on top of me. Stuff flew out of the wagon bed like somebody was back there shoveling.

"Would you believe . . . I'm gonna loose all my valuable merchandise!"

Me, I was worried we'd turn over and roll down the bank with the horse on top of us. "I don't care one bit about what's in the back."

The old mare clawed and pawed for all she was worth. Sparks flew like fireworks as her feet hit the rock. Suddenly she let out a squeal like her throat had been cut. The wagon slid faster. I couldn't wiggle my way out from under Spinsworthy.

He went right on mumbling about his goods. They rattled and banged as they fell out of the wagon bed. The tin ware bounced shoulder-high when it hit the rock.

The wagon hit the locust poles with a clunk. The left side rose higher and higher. I heard Spinsworthy's things and stuff fall out over the sideboards. They banged and rattled when they hit the rock. There was no way either of us could get up.

"We're gonna roll," I said.

We got our heads up enough to see over the front end of the wagon. The mare's rump was right in Spinsworthy's face. His red face had turned chalk white. Mine too, I guess.

For a long time, we seemed to hang in the air. The only sound was the pots and stuff rolling down the mountain. I couldn't get up anyway--with Spinsworthy on top of me. I reached out with my free hand and pushed against the rock for all I was worth. I knew I couldn't hold the thing up if it started to flip.

All at once, the high left side of the wagon started to fall back. Before I could say a word, the wheels hit the rock with a THUD. The rest of his things bounced out and rolled down the mountain.

Spinsworthy put me in mind of a cub bear as he crawled out the back of the wagon. The mare stood with all four feet spraddled out so wide her belly wasn't a foot off the rock. When I took hold of her bridle, I saw Spinsworthy climb down over the road bank, still on his hands and knees.

The wheels on the left side were bent all out of shape. I looked for them to fall apart at any time. I looked around. If any one had seen us they'd be laughing until I died.

Stuff rolled toward the creek. Then it tickled me. I laughed so hard my sides hurt. It took some doing to get the end gate back in the wagon while I tried to stand up on the rock.

With the wagon empty of people and stuff and the lower wheels against the locust log, the mare pulled it without any trouble. I led her past the rock.

The right shaft was bent where it had come down across the horse's back. "This is some mess I've got myself into." When I looked back Spinsworthy was climbing back into the road, with his arms full, and he had a big pot on his head.

It took the better part of an hour to gather up all the things. Spinsworthy fitted every piece in its place after he'd finished cleaning it with some part of his shirt.

"I think the wheels are busted," I said, pointing to the left side of the wagon. "Spokes loose on both of'em."

"Would you believe . . . some of my good and valuable mercantile went floating off."

I walked around looking the wheels over good. Both on the left side had big flat places. It looked like half the spokes were loose on the smaller front wheel. The rear wheel on the other side was warped all out of shape; it left a track like a snake.

"How'll we get this wagon back to the store?" I said.

Spinsworthy climbed back into the seat and picked up the reins "We've got traveling to do. I've got stops to make. Gitty-up."

The wagon rolled rough. When both flat places happened to hit the ground at the same time, it felt like the wheels were square; the whole thing bounced in the air. The warped wheels on the right side looked like they would fall over every time they made a round. The shaft pointed a foot above the mare's head. I just knew the whole thing would fall apart at any time.

Thirty minutes later we crossed the top of the ridge. The road was much better there. The wagon didn't ride near as rough in the sandy dirt. We stopped at a ford in the creek for the mare to drink.

Spinsworthy climbed in the back and worked on his things.

I saw smoke curling up through the trees ahead. At least we might get some help there.

Among a pile of boulders not twenty feet off the road, someone had built a house out of sawmill slabs. The rocks holding up the corners all leaned every which-a-way.

There wasn't any dogs or even chickens in the yard. I thought nobody lived there, until I saw three little kids on the porch. They looked to be five years old or younger.

"These folks haven't had nothing brought to them since early last winter." Spinsworthy grinned, greedy-like.

"Why don't they go to the store?" I said.

"The old man's dodging the law."

"What it is they want him for?"

Spinsworthy didn't answer. He climbed down from the seat and waddled toward the house.

Two of the children stared out from under a line of ragged clothes hanging from the porch sill. I didn't know if they'd never seen a wagon before, or if they were wondering how we were able to keep this one rolling.

"Hello, hello, the house. Elmer C. Spinsworthy come-a-calling."

The children never moved an eyelash. I had to look two more times to make sure they were really there. "Say there, is the woman of the house to home?" Spinsworthy said, putting his right foot up on the edge of the porch.

The kids stared straight ahead. A few minutes later a small woman stepped out from behind the chimney. She walked to the edge of the porch and looked at Spinsworthy. "Shore is."

"My fair lady," Spinsworthy said, pointing toward the wagon. "I've come here at much trouble and expense to bring you this good and valuable mercantile."

She walked straight to the wagon. "First off, I need a poke of salt."

"Would you believe . . . I thought of that when I left the city."

She didn't stop talking or moving until she had the sack of salt in her hands, holding it like a baby. "A sack of coffee, some soda, flour, and for sure, a sack of dried beans."

From the way she spoke, I could tell that she was scared there wouldn't be enough money. I'd never thought what it must be like to eat anything without seasoning.

Dad wouldn't set down at the table unless the salt and pepper shakers were right in front of him. When Aunt Nica cooked something the old-timey way, with herbs and the like, Dad would say it was all right. Then he'd lay the salt and pepper to it. If it was acorn or pumpkin bread, he'd cover it with butter and jelly or syrup.

"Would there be anything else?" Spinsworthy held up some little fancy plates.

The woman looked at the children. Their faces never moved, but their eyes told a sad story. Like me, they had seen that the woman didn't buy anything sweet except a small sack of sugar. For sure, there wouldn't be enough for them to poke their fingers in and suck.

While Spinsworthy pranced around showing off his wares, I unbuttoned my shirt and slid a poke of stick candy in right above my belt. "This looks like seventy-five cents worth to me; I'll make their eyes light up." I said it loud enough for Spinsworthy to hear, but he was so busy talking he couldn't.

"Anything for your man?" Spinsworthy said. "I've got some hair growth medicine that'll grow hair on a hoe handle."

I looked at the kids' faces. They never moved, but I knew their eyes hadn't missed what I'd done.

"Did you fetch the powder and lead?" The woman said, under her breath.

I could tell the children wanted to talk--I was afraid they'd come for the candy and Spinsworthy would think I'd stole from him. He wasn't about to pay me for the trip anyway. We'd be walking any minute. As quick as I could, I hurried around to the side of the house where the chimney stood. The candy fit on the ledge where the chimney narrowed down. There, no animal could reach it and I was sure they'd find it by the time we were out of sight.

"Them folks sure hungry for salt," I said to Spinsworthy when we were back in the wagon.

"Would you believe . . . I made me good money there."

"What's the law after the man for?"

"Would you believe . . . they claimed he burned a church."

"Did he? You reckon?"

"Probably not, but it's the easiest way to get a body sent to the work house."

"Well, I figure they'll make out somehow." I looked back at the house. The poke of candy was gone. I could see a grin on the kids' faces.

The next house wasn't more than a half a mile farther on up the valley. A log house with a wide porch stood between two big chestnut oaks.

I remembered it from the other trip, it being the only house I'd ever seen with a chimney in the back.

I knew Mr. Ralph Barringer lived here by himself. He hardly ever went to town or had a visitor--that's all I knew about him.

A while back, Reek and some of us boys had been on our way to the Hooper Bald to go hunting. We hadn't stopped at the place. "Shaw, shaw. That old man, he ax'd too many questions." Reek had said, picking up speed as we passed the house.

I knew Reek didn't like to tarry none when he was going hunting or on his way fishing. Still and all, Reek dearly loved to talk, so I had said, "What's wrong with that?"

"Shaw, he's deef as a dead dog."

Spinsworthy pulled the wagon right up to the house, like there was nothing wrong with the wheels. "Elmer C. Spinsworthy, come-a-calling."

Mr. Barringer came out of the house. His bushy gray hair stuck up in every direction. He walked straight to the wagon, his eyes fixed on the wheels, "Where did you'ens wreck?"

I couldn't help laughing while Spinsworthy tried to point out his good and valuable mercantile. Mr. Barringer reached over the wagon bed and picked up a sack of sugar. "What's this worth?"

"Would you believe . . . fine ground sugar. White as snow."

Barringer picked up a brown burlap sack of coffee beans. "You say a bugger got you? Yeah, you're gonna go slow. You won't get fur on them busted wheels."

Spinsworthy tried his best to show off everything in the wagon bed. He'd wipe it with his sleeve and hold it up for Mr. Barringer to see. If Mr. Barringer caught a word Spinsworthy said, he never let on. He went right on asking questions, and talking a mile a minute. "Don't see how them wheels stay on--why, the camber is all gone and the spokes are loose. You'll be walkin directly."

Climbing down off the seat, I walked to the branch that ran by the house and laid down to drink. Their voices carried on the water--sounded like two buzz saws. Holding back the laughter made my ribs sore.

"Tire'll run off'n that wheel a'fore you get outta rock throwing distance," Mr. Barringer said, when I got back to the wagon. "Where aire you'ens headed?"

"Would you care for one of these good pots?" Spinsworthy said.

"I see, all the way to Lots. That's a fur piece on a busted wheel."

"Could I interest you in a kitchen knife? Fine German steel."

"You'll bet your life. Will Gorman can fix any wagon wheel. Onliest thing is, he lives way over yander on Cold Cabin Creek."

"Look at all these good and valuable things in the wagon bed."

"Say you intend to turn your wagon into a sled? Hell fire! You'll need some runners."

On and on they went, neither paying any mind to the other. I waited while they sorted it all out

"How much did you say this here is?" Mr. Barringer held up a horse collar

"Two dollars, would you believe . . . a real steal."

"Used collars, you want'a swap for a wagon wheel?"

Spinsworthy turned his head in my direction. "Would you believe that?"

"I ain't got no wagon wheel," Mr. Barringer said. "Hell fire, you need four anyway. Where is it your heading?"

I held both my hands out, palms up. My sides hurt again from holding back the laughter. I wanted to go sit on the porch and watch and listen, but there was only one chair, and it had at least six pillows in it. Mr. Barringer probably wouldn't like it none. I jumped off the wagon and went back to the branch.

For the next half hour, I looked through the polished rocks in the branch for a gemstone of some kind. I sort'a have a knack for finding them. I hadn't found anything, except a few rust coated garnets, when I saw Mr. Barringer walking back toward the house. He set leaned back against the wall by the time I got even with the porch. "You idjets ain't going nowhere on them wheels."

Spinsworthy was sorting the things out in the big leather valise and muttering when I got into the seat. "Would you believe he's as deaf as a lard bucket?"

We hadn't gone out of sight of the house when we came to the first place where we had to ford the creek. When we reached the water's edge the left front wheel hit a boulder. The wheel flew into smithereens. The wagon dropped so quick I was sure Spinsworthy was going over the front-end gate.

The mare stopped right there. "Gitty-up." Spinsworthy clucked and clucked to her; but she wouldn't budge. I saw right off she didn't intend to pull the wagon another foot. Nor could a body blame her; she'd had a rough day. I made it a point not to get tickled any more; my ribs wouldn't take it.

Back at the house, Mr. Barringer sat in his chair leaned back against the wall. You would have thought he was asleep, but my guess was, he was laughing at us.

"Would you believe the luck?" Spinsworthy said, staring down into the water. "I guess it's now time for old pat and turner."

"Who's that?"

"Pat the ground and turn the corners. Hoofin it."

I was glad he hadn't lost his wits. Dad would have been raising mortal hell if he'd been through what we had. Then, Dad wouldn't ever have got in such a mess.

Then, my eye caught a long, slim, sourwood sapling in the laurel thicket down the creek. I had heard Dad and Reek talk about how a body could get home on three wheels, by making a runner for one wheel. Spinsworthy hadn't moved since the wheel busted.

I took one of the axes from the wagon bed and jumped over to the creek bank. The ax being new, it wasn't long before the sapling hit the ground.

Spinsworthy was still setting there, looking down into the water, when I finished chopping the runner.

An hour later, I had the wagon jacked up and the big wheel from the back put on the front. I put the sourwood pole under the back axle and tied the end to the wagon brake with a piece of new rope from Spinsworthy's things.

"Maybe we can get out of the creek," I said "If that mare will pull the thing."

Spinsworthy didn't move a muscle or say a word as I took the mare's reins and led her out of the creek.

He came alive once we had all three wheels and the runner on dry ground. "Would you believe . . . a body could drown back there."

I held my hand on my britches leg where the water had wet them. "Lord help my time! It ain't much over knee deep."

My problem was how to turn the thing around without losing the runner or putting the wobbly wheels in such a bind they fell off. We came to a small meadow up the road a ways. Ever so carefully, I led the mare in a big circle. When we got back to the creek, Spinsworthy was on his knees staring over the edge of the wagon bed into the water.

"If we get this heap back to town at all," I said, "it'll be dark-thirty."

"Would you believe . . . I've got all this good and valuable mercantile to take care of."

It didn't come to me how much we looked a fright until we got even with Mr. Barringer's place.

"How fur did you'ens get?" he called from his seat. "I told you them wheels was a'gonna fall off. Aire you'ens drunk?"

For once Spinsworthy didn't have an answer. Me, I was too worried about the big rock ahead, to care. As our luck would have it, we'd fall off the bluff and roll down right in front of the feed store. This time of day the place would be full of people to give us a ribbing. They would most likely call me Wobbly-Wheel, Spoke-Head, or some other silly thing, the rest of my life.

"Would you believe this mess? Would you believe this? Would you believe . . ."

"It could be worse," I said. "This wagon will fall apart any time."

The children at the slab house sat and stared as we came by. I waved when I saw the poke of candy in the little girl's lap. They waved back, but didn't bring their hands up more than a few inches. It made me feel good.

There wasn't no use to fret about it. I led the mare onto the big rock as if I knew what I was doing. I'll never know for a fact. It could have been the wagon wheels running against the locust poles, or the sourwood runner digging. That old wagon didn't slide an inch on the big rock. It most likely was the runner, for it made a gad-awful noise as it tried to dig into the granite. I know they could have heard it over in the next county.

Once we turned on to the main road, I felt for the first time that we might make it back to the feed store. Looking back at the crooked tracks we made, I shuddered. They might call me Snake-Track, the rest of my born days. I stopped the mare just around the bend from the feed store. I thought about rigging me up some pine limbs and dragging them to wipe out the wagon tracks. It wasn't no use; the runner was cutting too deep into the ground. At least it didn't make that awful sound in this loose dirt.

"Wagon-Runner, or Wobbly or Broke-Spoke or something like that," I said. "That's probably what my friend Ceece will call me forever. No, he'd make some kind of motion with his hands like a wheel wobbling, to pester me. Whatever he did, he would show me no mercy."

Spinsworthy didn't answer my mumbling; he just climbed back into the seat, pretty as you please, and commenced rubbing a pot with his shirttail. "Would you believe . . ." he said, "I can probably sell a bunch at the feed store if there's a crowd."

The mare got restless. Bad as I dreaded facing them, I picked up the lead rope and started toward the feed store. "Well," I said, mainly to myself. "Here goes nothing."

As we came into sight, I could tell from the trucks and wagons that there were plenty of people at the feed store. I didn't see our truck. There was no way to make a quick get-away.

I wanted to go slow, but the mare was stepping on my heels. She must have wanted to be rid of us. A body sure couldn't blame her.

I mumbled to myself, "We got one big wheel on the front, which makes the front of the wagon lean to the right. The runner on that same side makes the rear end lean bad to the left. Besides, I can kick every wheel on it apart barefooted. I've never seen a little boy's homemade wagon look this funny."

Spinsworthy paid no mind to me. He went right on spitting and polishing.

We were within a hundred feet of the store. They would pour out of there any minute and start ragging us. Then somebody would say something funny like "Ol'-Draggin-Wagon," and I'd have to tote the remembrance to my grave

It hit me like a light. I hung the lead rope on the mare's harness and darted around the building. By the time I got to the other side, the mare had stopped right in front of the door. I looked back as the last person filed out the door.

"Evening all, Elmer C. Spinsworthy come-a-calling. I've got a wagon load of good and valuable mercantile."

The crowd kept their eyes on the wagon. I could have walked right up behind them.

"What hit you?" one farmer said. "It must'a been a doosey."

212

"Must have run into a sea of troubles," another said.

The feed store man walked right up and put his foot on the big wheel. I knew he was about to tear Spinsworthy up.

I wanted to watch and hear what was going to take place. Instead, thirty minutes later I walked into the poolroom.

"Where you been?" Dad said, looking at my dry but wrinkled britches.

"Took a little wagon ride."

Dad went back to talking to the man on his left. I walked back out on the street thinking about all the jokes I had heard about traveling salesmen. One thing I can say about Spinsworthy: he was a true drummer.

MOUNTAIN'S A'FIRE -- Men from Boys

It rained very little that spring, and turned off dry the first of July. Blades on the corn stalks rolled up no bigger than a kid's finger.

"By fall the woods will look like the depths of hell," Dad said, while we stood out in front of the house and watched the blazing sun set over Joanna Bald.

"Shaw," Reek said, "You right about that. They like a tinder box now."

Reek came to our house early every day. Him and Dad had dug a ditch from way up the creek to water Mama's garden.

Mama didn't like to water her garden that way. She claimed: "Flooding the ground like that leaches all the manure and fertilized so far down in the ground the plants cain't reach it."

"Well you can sure bet, we won't raise a tater bigger than a guinea egg if we don't," Dad said.

"You won't have to worry much longer," I said. "Where we could dip up a five-gallon lard bucket full of water from the creek before, you cain't get a thimble full."

214

"What puts the most worry on me," Dad said, "if'en it don't rain these woods will burn down by late fall."

Reek lived by himself and took at least one meal a day at our house. Mama set a place for him just like the rest of us. This had gone on as long as I could recall. In season, he kept us in fish and game to pay his keep, and he liked her cooking, I reckon.

No rain came in July or August. The leaves on the dogwood and poplar were the first to turn brown and fall. Then the beach and locust leaves wilted and fell. By the last week in August the oaks had commenced to shed. The fields were so dusty Dad kept us out of them. "No need to hoe them crops; they done and burnt up."

Reek brought up an old quarrel that has gone on here in these mountains for many a year. "Shaw, Folks ought to burn the woods in the spring and early summer, like the old-timers did."

"You're right," Dad said. "The leaves didn't rot this spring and summer like common. In places, they're waist deep. The old-timers took that into account and made ready for times like these. They took control of when the woods burnt and didn't leave it to chance."

"Shaw, there weren't no underbrush back then. I recollect when a body could ride a horse through the woods, anywhere he took a notion."

The pasture grass and weeds stopped growing everywhere except down near the stream bed and I had to graze the stock along the creek bank. Most days, I went to the river, cut tall ragweeds, and carried them home. It saved time and worry from standing around watching the stock hunt for a bite here and yonder.

Three days later Dad and Reek took Ceece with us up to the cornfield. Like Reek, Ceece spent a lot of time at our house. Ceece was something over a year younger than me, and he took a lot of looking after.

Dad unrolled some blades on a corn stalk. "We might as well cut these tops and pull the fodder. There won't be any corn, to speak of, in these patches."

When we had all the shocks standing on the dusty hillside, Dad pointed to a long cove on Blood Mountain that was brown as shoe leather. "That stand of poplars looks like it commonly does in late winter."

"Shaw, there won't be enough mast this year to feed one old bushy-tail."

"What don't starve," Dad said, "will get burned out if it don't rain."

"Shaw, I don't recollect hit ever bein this dry a'fore. Why, a body won't need no pole to catch fish; they'll be a'walkin."

"Reek," Dad said, "we might as well go sign up to help fight the timber fires. Them rangers gonna need ever hand they can get."

Ceece kicked at a dirt clod. "What'd it pay?"

"Shaw, the pay is twenty-five cents an hour on giv-er-ment land and ten on private."

"They pay fifty cents a day for standby," Dad said. "You have to stay near the meeting point from ten in the morning til after dark."

Ceece put his hand on his hips. "Well, I won't go for no part of no fire fighting."

"Shaw, they'll concrete you and take you, if'en you're of age."

"He means conscript," Dad said.

"What does 'conscript' mean?" I said.

"It's the law here in these mountains," Dad said. "If they ask you to fight fire and you won't, they'll throw you in jail."

"Shaw, for a fact--them town loafers are done dodging the poolroom, a'feared they'd be called on to help."

"Can I go?" I said.

"You're how old?" Dad said.

"Yeah," I said. He never could remember how old any of us were. I wanted to add: if the tobacco crop fails too, we'd need every cent we can lay our hands on. I held it back to mumble to myself later.

"Well, by golly," Ceece said, "I ain't a'goin to stay here and listen to them sisters of yourn all blamed summer by myself. I'll be the water boy."

"Come Monday morning," Dad said, "We'll go over to Miller's Mill and sign up."

The head ranger made Dad a Warden. He hired Dad and Reek to run a telephone wire up the creek to the store. They hung it on tree limbs, so the tower over on Raven's Cliff could keep in touch with folks here if fire broke out.

Wednesday night as we sat down to eat, Mama gave us the word: "They put off starting school until it rains. Most folks are afraid their little'uns going back and forth to school will get caught in a fire."

"Shaw, truth be known," Reek said, "they're trying to rake up enough victuals to make it through this winter, and need ever hand they can git."

Evenings are the worst time for a woods fire, so Dad told us not to be at the mill until ten in the mornings. He said we would stay until the dew fell at night. Reek put new handles in the axes and rakes as fast as he could whittle them out. He didn't mention fishing once, so that led me to think fire business was something to dread. Although the pay wasn't much, we had little to do. It kept me busy watching out for Ceece, and keeping him from foundering on soda pop and little round pies.

One hot evening as we sat on the porch of the mill, the phone rang. Dad picked it up. "Yeah. Yeah. I see. Yeah. Yeah, we're leavin."

Ceece looked at me. He was holding a soda pop in each hand. I pointed to the steps that Dad had just gone down.

Dad stood on the back of his truck and looked out over the men standing out in the road. "Men, it looks like the freight train up on Shake Rag set the woods on fire. This is the first fire some of you have been on. I intend to bring you back unhurt."

We loaded into Dad's truck. Our feet rested on a pile of fire rakes, axes, and shovels. The buckets that hung from the standards rattled so we couldn't hear ourselves think, let alone talk above the racket. Dad drove as fast as the old truck would run. We held onto the sideboards to keep from falling off.

Going up Shake Rag, the truck bounced over the big rocks. The tires squealed like a cut pig when they hit the next rock. Dad drove around a ridge high on the mountain and slid to a stop in the head of a hollow that was full of smoke.

Like yellow jackets boiling out of their nest, the men came off the truck, each with a fire rake in his hand. They stood in front of the truck while Dad walked over to the road bank and stared into the smoke-filled hollow. I didn't know how to fight a fire so I held back and watched.

Dad turned to face us. "Men, this hollow acts like a funnel. The draft whips the wind up through it like a gale. Climb down and cut the fire off three hundred yards below here. Fan out and work your way out on the ridges."

Without a word, the men leapt off into the smoke-filled woods. Ceece followed me to the truck; the only rakes left had metal pipe handles and weighed at least fifteen pounds each. I picked one up and started for the woods. Ceece picked up the other rake and threw it down. He was untying a bucket when Dad walked up and took it out of his hand. "Get you a rake and hit them woods!"

Sweat and smoke caused our eyes to water like a spigot. You couldn't see more than the ground around your feet. Somehow, we found the men. They dug like there was no tomorrow--raked a swath in the earth some three feet wide in the dry ground. You couldn't see the fire below, but it crackled and popped to let us know it would soon be there.

As usual, Dad was already there; he pointed to me. "Go to the end of the line and cut a strip just like these men are doing. Rake all the way down to the fresh dirt."

"Don't you need a water boy?" Ceece said.

Dad went right on chopping at the roots of a pine stump. "Move your ass!"

We made our way to the end of the line, out on the side of the ridge. Out there, the smoke was not near as bad, and the leaves were not as thick. But the briars tore at our arms like barbwire. For two hours we cut and raked, sweated and coughed. Blisters formed and burst. The fire crept within twenty feet of our line. We watched every place where it looked like the fire might cross the line. The light from the flames made the work easier, and we could see ten feet ahead through the smoke. We raked as fast as we could ever time the flames started across the firebreak.

After full dark, Dad walked through the smoke and ashes to where we were. "It's held. Get your buckets and fetch some water so we can mop up and go home. Don't drink enough to founder."

Ceece threw down his rake "Well, by golly, he's finally going to let us tote water. At least now, we can get a drink."

"You better take that rake back to the tuck"

It was a quarter of a mile almost straight off to a branch a few feet wide. Ceece and I laid down and put our faces in the cool water. We found a small waterfall and filled the buckets. We climbed back toward where Lawrence and Jabo Spivey were digging around a smoldering chestnut stump. They looked at us and broke out laughing.

At first, I thought we had done something foolish, or else we were in the wrong place. Ceece turned toward me. His nose, mouth, eyes, and part of his cheeks and forehead were white. The rest of his face was black, covered with smut and ashes. His face looked like a saucer with black paint around it.

"What's so funny?" Ceece said.

I pointed to my face.

Ceece didn't laugh. He wiped his face with both hands.

When we got up near where they were, Jabo looked at me. "You look like you've been hit in the face with a pan of whitewash."

"And the other looks like--looks like--looks like a zebra." Lawrence added.

"Jabo, why are you digging around this stump?" I said, when the laughing stopped. "It's ten feet below the fire line."

Dad walked up about that time. "Chestnut and hemlock, as well as old oak stumps, burn all the way to the ends of their roots--sometimes forty or even fifty feet. If their roots pass under the firebreak we could have another fire."

For a while, I kept count of our trips to the branch, then I was so give out it didn't matter. A bucket full of water didn't go far toward putting out a fire in the hot, dry ground. Smoldering stumps were everywhere. We carried our buckets and dumped them where the men told us. Lawrence and Jabo made mud pies and packed them on the ends of roots that wouldn't stop burning.

It was near midnight and the moon had gone down over Weatherman Bald when word passed down to us. "Let's call it cured--cain't see--let's go home."

The men gathered in the road by the truck. Dad turned on the headlights. "Anybody hurt?"

There was no answer, although I saw some men rub places on their arms and legs. Dad motioned for the men to come closer. "Come on up here in the light, and let's take a look."

Dad looked over each man as they walked by. He spoke to every one, but I couldn't make out what it was he said. I hung back til last. Ceece picked at the blisters on his hands.

Dad looked over to where we stood. "Come on, up here, if you two can still walk."

The men laughed.

"I'm all right," I said.

"You two ought to do something about them faces," Dad said. "Load up."

Dad drove into town and parked in front of the bus station. It was the only place in town where you could get anything to eat after dark.

Dad walked in first and spoke to the cook. "Heat up the big skillet; I've got a hungry bunch of men."

Ceece ate two plates full, and between bites, he asked every man there except Dad: "How much money did I make? Was that government land or private? How come I had to use a rake with a pipe handle?"

Dad paid for the food that I know cost him more than he made that day. Ceece ate more than any two of the grown men.

Dad drove slower on the way back to the cove. He even went out of the way to let every man off as near his house as the truck would go.

Once we got to Rail Cove and parked at the house, we stood in the yard. Dad turned to Reek. "That was a small fire, maybe twenty acres or less. We're apt to get a big one if rain don't come soon. How do you feel?"

Reek was getting on in years and he had a bout with the shingles almost every winter, but you'd never know it from the way he acted. "Shaw, a fresh dip of snuff and I'll be right thar."

By the middle of October, the mountains looked like the dead of winter. Only the laurels along the creeks still had leaves; they were rolled up like little green cigars. There hadn't been even a wisp of a cloud in the sky in over two weeks. We had been on at least four fires every week, but none that lasted more than part of a day.

The last Saturday of the month, fire struck Long Ridge--that's what we call the four-thousand-foot-high mountains--which runs all the way from Frog Mountain in Tennessee and Georgia to way back in the Great Smoky Mountains. From far off the high peaks and deep gaps make it look like a long, narrow set of jagged stair steps.

Once the call came in, Dad gathered us in front of the mill, and I saw the worry in his face. "Men, it's hit Long Ridge. As you know, it runs southeast to northwest, and the south wind has blown for three days. We gotta hurry and you've got to be extra careful on this one."

All of us piled into the truck and Dad drove like a bat out of hell, toward the state line. I could see the smoke ten miles before we reached the base of Long Ridge. High on the mountain, a patch of ivy covered part of the ridge crest. It looked to cover about ten acres all together. All at once, it burst into a ball of flames two hundred feet high. By the time we drove around the next curve and looked up, nothing was left except smoking bare scrubs.

Ceece shook my arm. "There's a right smart more smoke than the fires we've been on."

"A heap more fire too," One of the old-timey firefighters allowed. I saw a frown come on the faces of the old firefighters. Some pointed while others dropped their heads.

The truck slid to a halt beside a small branch, a half a mile below the crest of Long Ridge. I looked at the big boulders that lined the streambed. In normal times, the branch would have been a river.

Dad was at the back of the truck before any of the men got off. "Men, climb to that rocky ridge top and start your cut just to the right of the peak. Hopefully, the fire will slow down once it gets above that ring of broom sage and brush along the bottom of the ridge. It's our best shot to stop this thing."

"If we can stop it on that ridge top," a voice from the truck said, "we'll be home for dinner. If not, all hell will be to pay."

Dad led the way to the peak of the ridge. Smoke choked us as we gathered on the crest. It was maybe a minute before Dad spoke. "Half of you go down one side and half the other; rake as wide a break as you feel you have time to, but don't get caught."

Ping! Bang! Clang! Whang! The sounds of men and tools as we chopped, raked, yanked, and dug among the boulders. The noise we made didn't drown out the roar of the fire as it got closer and closer. By the time we got down below the rocks, the air was filled with white-hot sparks. Hot wind burned our skin like someone had opened the door on an oven. It was so hot and dry the sweat dried before it reached our clothes, yet our eyes watered, which caused streaks on all our faces.

I was working below Ern Tally and above Ceece, when Ern came down toward me. I had never seen a look like he had on his face. "We'll know in a minute if the thing's going to hold. Cut your line off toward that hollow. We cain't let the fire get below us."

I liked to work with Ern. He'd been fighting fires all his life. He knew a right smart about what a fire would do and how to plan where to make a firebreak. That way, we didn't beat our brains out digging in a rock bar or laurel thicket.

226

When I got half way down the mountain, I saw fire leap through the pine tree tops off to my left. Dad came by us in a lope. He ran on up the mountain without saying a word. In the brown grass down in the flats it was hard to cut a firebreak. We pulled and tugged as hard as we could, until we cut a break all the way to the branch. Ceece and two other firefighters laid face-down in the water and drunk with their faces all the way under.

"How far is it to the next road that crosses this mountain?" I said.

Ern took of his cap and rubbed his dirty hand through his hair. "I don't recall there being one."

We stood in the road and watched the mountain like there was some great thing about to take place. The sky was so full of smoke it was hard to see the ridge line. What should have been a bright fall sun put me in mind of a dingy yellow ball.

"How long til the sun sets?" I said.

Ern took of his cap again. "By rights, there's better than five good hours left."

The smoke grew thinner when the fire reached the peak where we had cut the firebreak. Red flames glowed through the thick haze, but they were not as bright or high as they had been. Even Ceece stood with us without saying anything. I walked toward the branch and said to myself: "Dad's on that mountain. Where at?"

We all saw it at the same time. Flames more'n three hundred feet high shot out of a deep hollow and landed fifty yards on the other side of the break. The wind fanned them like a giant set of bellows. I heard Ern from behind me. "Damn my time, it jumped the plaguid firebreak."

Two others kept saying, "Damn, son-of-a-bitch. Son--of--a--bitch!"

Every man stood with his rake in his hand and stared at the growing fire. I felt more uneasy about Dad. Without thinking, I walked toward the fire.

"Whur you a goin?" Ceece said, by the time I got to the water.

"Look for Dad."

"He's a comin down the road, yonder."

Dad counted heads as he came toward us almost in a trot. "Men, it looks like we've got a jump."

A voice from behind me said, "I don't see how the fire broke through. I dug that stretch myself."

Another voice added. "How it leapt all the way out'a that hollow is beyond me. It must be well over a hundred yards."

"Son-of-a-bitch."

"There may be a snake in the wood pile," Dad said. "I'll take the truck and go around the road to where Reek and the others are. We'll meet in that low gap yonder and try again. Watch yourselves. Don't get caught where you cain't out run the flames."

"Dag-nab-it, what's the use," Ceece said as we crossed the branch. "If'en somebody is a'settin fires ahead of us; we're pissin in the wind."

When we got to the low gap, Reek and the others' faces were covered as much with worry as with sweat. The smoke and flames reached higher than ever and roared like thunder.

I walked up beside one man, who answered before I asked. "It jumped our end of the line too."

We raked the leaves and roots back while some men jumped down the hollow and went to work. Dad came to us thirty minutes later; he held a two-gallon can in each of his hands as he walked up to where we were. "Take this lamp oil and back-set the line Reek and the others cut. Dribble out the oil slow; the cans got to last you all the way off the mountain. Use a pine top for a torch. Be careful. Ceece, you go with me; we'll do the same down this side."

"Goody," Ceece said. "Goody, goody."

I started my fire in the gap, and it spread fast, like a snake crawling over hot coals. I raked with one hand while the wind blew the fire back toward the firebreak. Other times, it caught so fast I moved right before the flames hit my leg. On the steep slopes, I sprinkled a little oil so the flames would burn down hill, then chased them as they raced back up. This job was harder than digging a firebreak and a damn sight hotter. "I wish I could see

Ceece," I said, over and over to myself. "I'll wager you he'll mumble like a June bug in a jar."

When I caught up with the diggers, there was a good-sized fire behind me. A man helped me fire the last hundred yards.

"Thanks." I said.

"Never make mention of it."

"Do you think this line will hold?"

His face dropped a little, like a worry had come over him. "We thought the last one would hold."

"Maybe Ceece needs some help with his back-set; I'm going back over there." I said.

A voice from across the creek bellowed out: "Ceece is apt to get mad and set fire on the wrong side, just for spite."

"You be keerful," a voice from somewhere behind me said.

It took me less than thirty minutes to cross the top of the ridge. All along the firebreak, the ground on the south side was scorched. Ceece had done better than I figured.

I climbed along the top of a rock cliff, and looked for a way down. I saw Ceece working at the base. He pulled at the brown grass that grew up to the timber's edge.

Six men that I had seen down in Wayside set under a big June apple tree up against the foot of the mountain. The leaves were gone, but a few apples hung on the limbs of the old tree. Three of the men peeled and ate the apples that laid on the ground.

That whole bunch of men hung around town most of the time, except on cattle sale day. What little work I had ever seen them do was tending the gates for a few hours before the sale started.

"At least they could help us with the mopping up," I said to myself.

"Ha! Ha! He! Heee!" They pointed at Ceece. "That damn fool almost burned his britches off. If that's what they sent here to fight fire, it ain't no wonder the whole world's a'burnin. They might as well left them home with their mammies."

Ceece was thirty yards from the men, finishing his back-set. He did look funny with the left leg of his overalls burned near-about to his knee. Even from halfway up the rock cliff, I could see scratches and streaks of blood where briars had torn his leg.

"Haw-haw!" Another said. "Now that we're here the baby hick can go home to his mama; let us men do the work."

I knew they didn't have any idea how short a fuse Ceece had, or else they would be on their feet. Ceece came at them with his eyes bulged out like a mad bull. He headed straight for the June apple tree. "You lard-asses stand up and I'll part your hair with this rake!"

Any one of the fellows would make two of Ceece. They were at least ten years older, or better. I knew he was fixing to wade into them--I ran halfway down over the cliff and jumped--Ceece had the fire rake drawn back when I tumbled onto the grass. Five of the men scrambled around behind the tree.

One big man jumped up in Ceece's face. "Why, boy, I'll feed you that rake and slap you a'windin!"

It scared me that he thought he could bluff Ceece with his size and talk--the man was about to get himself a necktie made out of a rake handle. Most likely get his head cut off with that fire rake to boot.

I got to Ceece right as he started his downswing with the rake. I shoved him forward enough so that the blade of the rake went across the man's shoulder. The handle hit him on the side of his neck hard enough to bring the man to his knees.

Ceece looked at me. "Damn, you made me miss!"

The other men scurried to find and get hold of something to fight with. Without thinking, I kicked two of their rakes down into the tall grass. By this time, Ceece was wound tighter than a cheap watch. It was hard to tell if he was going to come after me, or hit the man again, or what.

"Come on Ceece," I said. "Lave'em be!"

"Hell fire! I mean to let them pussel-gutted town-apes have all they want of me!"

Backing up four or five steps, I charged into Ceece with my shoulder. It caught him off balance and I carried him toward the branch in a dead run. Then I threw him in the biggest pool of water in the branch. Three of the men from our crew came down before I let Ceece's head come up for air.

"What's all the commotion about?" Ern said.

I shoved Ceece's head back down in the water, lifted it out so he could breathe every once in a while, and told them what had happened.

Ern laughed. "He's probably cooled off enough so he won't set the woods afire again by breathing on it. Let him up."

We heard Dad's truck coming around the curve. I led Ceece back to the road. Dad handed me a five-gallon lard bucket full of food. He stared at Ceece, then turned to the rest of us. "We've got some help on the way. The women sent food."

Ceece looked across the branch at the town men until I stuffed a peanut-butter sandwich in his mouth.

"Ain't you got nothin better'n this choke-butter?" Ceece said, "I won't even eat this stuff at home."

A loud roar came from the mountain when the two fires ran together. Every eye stared at a steep hollow where the main fire raced toward the head to meet the fire Ceece had set. Both fires died out near the top like a wet blanket had been thrown over them. The flames were gone; the smoke fell to the ground. It looked like the whole sky was filled with smoke, except over that hollow. I saw the dead and down timber that filled it, plain as the palm of my hand.

I looked at Dad "What in the world?"

"Watch'er blow any time now." Ern said.

"The fire it burned up the air in the hollow," Ern said. "You watch in just a min--"

K-E-R B-O-O-M! It was louder than dynamite going off in a quarry. The mountain trembled. The shock knocked all of us back a few steps. It rained fire a quarter of a mile in every which way you looked, like the end of time. Sticks big as cordwood flew like flaming torches. They sailed well past the fire line we had dug.

"Looks like the gates of hell just blew open," Ern said.

Dad took off his hat and pointed almost straight up, at a low gap. "It's hard but it's fair. Grab your rakes and head for that low saddle; maybe we can cut it off there. I'll drive around and get Reek's crew started up there. You be careful. You see now, how a man can get killed fighting fire. Come on Ceece, get in the truck."

I looked across to where the men from town had been laying under the June apple tree. Fire covered every inch of ground around it. The men weren't nowhere in sight.

"Where do you reckon the men from town are?" I said.

"The last account I had of'em," somebody said from up the road, "they were under that apple tree."

I grabbed my rake and started out behind the firefighters. We ran a half a mile up the road, and looked for an easy way to climb the mountain again. The mountain was steeper and higher that deep in the Smokies. We climbed slower, for we had to stop every two hundred yards to catch our wind. At least this low gap was far enough from the fire that the awful smell of burning pine wood didn't cause my nose to water. I hunkered down close to the ground and got me a breath of fresh air.

By the time Dad, Reek, and the others reached the gap, we had a good break dug across the wide saddle.

Dad counted heads, then got out in front of us. "We'll be fighting this thing after dark, more apt than not; be extra careful."

"What about help?" one old firefighter said.

"I reckon," Dad said, "the rangers manning the towers can see, with the firestorm, that the fire's bigger than ever. They'll do what they can about rounding up help. They got a telephone. We don't."

"What about the bunch from town?" Ern said, "there were six of them."

Dad grinned. "I saw them a'walkin, up the road. Their clothes burned near-bout off'em. One had a burn hole in his hat big as a teacup. Some of their clothes were still smoking."

Dad handed Ceece another can of lamp oil. I looked for Ceece to try to get out of that job, but he didn't say nothing. He was too busy grinning and giggling that silly giggle. "Heee-hee. Heee-hee."

Reek was squatted down like he was give out, or troubled. He had to be the oldest one there. He took the tin snuffbox out of his bib pocket and tapped the lid. "Shaw, I'm pert-near out of snuff."

Dad reached into his coat pocket and handed him a fresh can. Reek kept the off side of our truck coated with snuff stains, and the dashboard lined with cans. Dad always made sure Reek had a good store of snuff on hand.

Reek jerked his hat back on his bald head and jumped up. He worked like he had rested for days. The men followed, and soon we raked and back-set like the times before. Ceece didn't try to hang back like common.

We started in the gap, and dug the firebreak down both sides. It was below the main top, which kept the smoke above us for a hundred feet or so. Once we got down under the top of the mountain, it looked like the whole world was on fire. I back-set and tried to stay up with the men doing the raking, but I wasn't sure where all the fire was.

I saw the fire coming from my left. I worked as fast I could. When the main fire met the little fire I had set, firestorms rained everywhere. None of them was as powerful as the one that blew everything out of the hollow. In the low gap that Dad called a saddle, the ground was loose, and that made digging easier. We soon had a break fifteen feet wide. The fire traveled slower as it burned downhill. I felt this time that our lines would hold for sure.

Boom! Boom! Kerboom! Every time the fire blew out in a hollow, it made a different sound. Bo-oom! K-boom!

"Sounds like a young war." Ern came up to where I was. He wiped his face on a red bandana. "It may take a rain to put this damn thing out."

When we were another quarter of the way down the mountain, a man from Reek's crew ran by us. "Run, boys run, hit's jumped the line again!"

"Where?" Ern said.

"Not a hundred yards from the top! On your side!"

"I don't see how in the world it could have jumped near the top. We dug that line good!" Ern nodded in the direction the man went. "Besides, it was back-set, blame-near an hour ago."

The road was full of trucks and men when we crossed the branch. There must have been twenty-five in all.

A man in green uniform and badge talked to Dad. "Where do you think we should try to cut it off this time?"

"There's no natural break for a long ways now," Dad said. "It's a long shot but I'd try that point near that lone white pine, a half a mile ahead of the fire. It'll leave a quarter-mile gap between us and the fire by the time we can climb up there."

"You heard him!" the ranger man said. "Let's fight some fire!"

With the smoke and haze, and the sun setting, dark was coming fast. Dad had to walk right up to each of us to count heads. Only when the treetops burst into flames could I see all the men.

Dad, Reek, and the ranger man talked in low voices when we met under the tall white pine.

"Do you believe this fire's getting help from somebody?" the ranger man said.

"That's my thinking," Dad said.

"Shaw yes," Reek said. "In my time I've seed fire cross a break, but I never seed one take off bigger'n it was in the first place."

"We did have a firestorm that blew fire all over the mountain," Dad said. "It covered at least a good quarter of a mile in every direction. It reset on the far side, well past the second break we dug. Still, I found gaps back there a ways that hadn't burnt. It sure makes a body wonder."

"Have you seen any strangers hereabouts?" the ranger man said.

"No," Dad said. "We've been too busy to look for sign."

With the help of the new men, the line was cut deeper and wider and a lot faster. Two men with tanks on their backs did the back-setting. They sprayed fire out of the muzzle of a long tube.

"Where is your Dad?" Ern said, as we walked down the mountain to take our place at the head of the line. "He generally comes by every little bit."

I never let on, but I knew Dad was somewhere on the mountain looking for whatever it was that kept setting the fire across our line.

By the time we got to the road, night had come over the mountain. The streaks of fire glowed like ribbons through the smoke. Some raced along like bellows were behind them, while others crept along. We stood in the road and watched like it was a giant fireworks show. The only sound that came from any of us was coughing as the fresh air tried to clean out throats and lungs.

"Earlier we saw all manner of game dodge and dart away from the fire," Ern said. "Now nothing, they must know the thing is out of hand."

Ceece muttered to himself, first about the pay then about the men under the apple tree. "If you hadn't caught me, I'd have made firefighters out of that bunch of town bums."

I scooped a handful of water out of the branch and threw it in his face. "I have to keep cooling you off."

"Damn!" one, of the new men said, "look a'yonder!"

"That's well beyond the place where we came down, back-setting." Ern said.

We stared at the flames a quarter of a mile to our right. "That part of Long Ridge looks like a crosscut saw standing on its end," Ceece said. "It gets so rocky you cain't dig for shit."

"Do you reckon something rolled down across the line?" I said.

"Could be," Ern said. "Let's hurry, maybe we can head it off!"

That fire didn't start slow and build up; flames jumped like the mountainside was covered with gasoline or gunpowder. By the time we reached the foot of the mountain, fire was halfway to the top. Flames swirled above the treetops, a hundred feet high. Where's Dad? I said, to myself.

"Let's cut it off, way out ahead of the fire." Ern said.

"Yonder is a gap." Another firefighter pointed three-quarters of a mile to our right.

Dad did not like to give fire any more ground than he had too. "Where is Dad, anyway?"

Most of us that had been here from the start had to pull up by trees and use our hands to help our legs keep going.

When we reached the low gap, I looked for Reek's crew. We couldn't set a backfire if they were in front of us. The fire'd got harder to fight all the time.

When we talked about it, one of the new men leaned on his rake. "Let the damn thing burn itself out."

"The hell you say!" Ern and two other men said at the same time.

"While you get started digging," I said. "I'll go look for Reek's crew--be back in time to back-set."

"Well, dag-nab it I'm goin too." Ceece said.

"You two be careful," Ern said. "We'll not back-set while you're out there."

"I'll--I'll go with you," Tib Shope said. "I'm a back-setter; they won't need me til we get back."

We couldn't take our eyes off the fire up ahead to watch where we were going at the same time. The huckleberry bushes reached to our waist, and tore at our legs. I didn't say a word to them, but we were headed straight into the fire. To find anyone in this thicket in the dark and smoke would be one of the wonders of all wonders.

Within a hundred yards of the fire the flames gave enough light to see through the thick smoke. There was no sign of Reek or any of his crew.

"What if we get lost?" Tib said.

"Hell fire," Ceece said, "get lost on top of a ridge. Besides if we go much further, we'll burn our asses off."

Our heads jerked around, each of us afraid we would somehow get trapped by the fire. We stood, not knowing what to do for several minutes. Tib's eyes looked like a sick calf's.

BOOM! We reeled backwards, from the blast off to our left. Flames jumped two hundred feet high as they raced out the tops of the dry pine trees in the hollow below. Wind from the flames sucked dry leaves and sticks from under out feet. They hit

241

us like rocks as they fell back down. Balls of fire shot out like thousands of roman candles going off at once. The thing was, these were not little balls of fire--whole treetops rained down around us.

Bang! Another blast rocked the woods. This time it had a tin ring to it--sounded like a brass cannon.

Ceece turned and looked back. "What? What? What? Wha-whaw-wauz-was that?"

"Something blew up." I said.

"Hell, I knowed that. What?"

"I don't have the foggiest notion. Run!"

"There'll be no need to back-set, now," Tib said. "Fire's everywhere."

"Damn it--run!"

The smoke was thick: couldn't see Ceece and Tib thirty feet away. Crash! Crash, crash. The treetops fell from the sky. "Run! Run! Run!" I yelled.

"We're right behind you," Ceece said.

"Keep yelling so we won't loose each other," I said. "And run!"

I made for higher ground--yelled every breath: "Run!"

They answered back, "Yeah--yeah!"

A few hundred yards up the mountain, when my breath gave out, I looked back. The fire had gained on us.

Five minutes later, we were in a field of big boulders. We slowed down as we crawled around and over the rocks.

"We're in deep shit," Ceece said as he bumped into me.

"This way," I said.

We climbed over the rocks until we made our way to just below the crest of the ridge. "At least we're on the side away from the worst of the fire."

Wind from the fire had sucked all the smoke from a quarter-acre spot. Ten feet below, a rock cliff overhung two boulders the size of truck cabs. "This way," I said.

The air trapped in the pocket between the rocks was fresh and still. We drank it in like water.

"Rake these leaves and brush away, down to the fresh dirt!" I said, throwing them out like a hen scratches. "Fill every crack with rocks and dirt."

Flames raced up the other side of the ridge. The sound was so loud it hurt our ears. I saw a big flat rock leaning against the cliff. Ceece saw it at the same time. We rolled it to the boulders and slid it on top of them like a roof. It wobbled, but it reached all the way across; inside, we had us a makeshift cave.

Once Tib made out what we were doing, he started to cry.

"Shut the hell up and pack them cracks with dirt." Ceece said.

"Do--Don't you'ens hear the fire a'comin?" Tib said.

"You'll feel it fry your hide if you don't get your ass in gear," Ceece said.

Tib helped pack the cracks with whatever we could put our hands on. He sobbed and mumbled to himself while he worked. "What if a burning tree falls on top of this thing? Hot fire'll crack these rocks down around us."

Lying on the ground inside, we packed the last cracks and raked the earth bare, tying to find some dampness. A foot deep there was none.

"At least the air in here is fresher than any we've breathed in a long time," I said.

I pulled Tib down between us and his crying slowed but he rattled on. "I feel hotter already. Maybe we should run--reckon they'll find our bones?"

"Shut up," Ceece said, "When I'm gone I don't give a crap what happens to my corpse."

"Bahaa! We'll smother to death!"

"Shut the hell up! You're a'burnin up too much air with that infernal crying."

The fire made all manner of strange sounds as it popped and cracked and fried all around our manmade cave. We sat up and packed dirt into any place where smoke could get in. After what felt like a lifetime, the sounds died down and the air inside got so bad we coughed and gasped.

My thoughts went back to the time when I was about five and got turned around and lost my way up on Tallow-Dip Creek. Right before I started to cry, I heard the faint whistle, "Scre-e-e-t," that Dad would give when he wanted to let you know where he was.

Folks had always guessed that Dad and Reek would die in the woods. Most likely, they would be found where they had waited for it to get light enough to see what the dogs had treed. Mama always feared they would drown trying to cross the Tennessee or the Nolchucky River after their dogs. Or else, they would get killed falling off a cliff one dark night trying to make their way out of the Linville Gorge.

Many a time I'd waited at the truck or camp for them, calling out with every signal I knew. Later, they'd walk up after pitch dark, quiet as ghosts.

The roar of the fire sounded like it was past us, and now all I could hear was the whimpering sound Tib made.

"Let's get the hell out of here," Ceece said.

I put my shoulder against the top rock and pushed it off. The air was full of smoke and ashes. The air in our manmade cave had been far better than this.

I had a terrible hankering to hurry and look for Dad and Reek. I took hold of Ceece and Tib's arms. "Let's run for it. Follow me, we're going to the road. Watch out for falling trees and run like hell!"

We held our breaths and ran straight down the mountain, dodging the burning stumps and snags. Halfway down, the air cleared some and we stopped to breathe the fresh air as it rose from the creek valley. We coughed at first, but the air in the little hollow was so clear you couldn't see much smoke.

"Let's stay here--the air is--"

The top fell out of a burned hemlock tree and hit the ground right behind us. Ceece and Tib passed me like their rear-ends were a'fire. We didn't stop until we reached the road. I caught my breath and ran up the road toward where Dad had parked the truck. Were Dad and Reek all right?

I rounded the curve. The road was full of men standing around. Something had happened.

Dad's truck blocked my view. I started to yell but didn't have the breath to make a sound. The three hundred yards left to go looked like a mile.

"Where's Dad?" I said to the first man I came too--one of the ones that stood out in front of Dad's truck.

"Wait right here," he said, then took hold of my arm.

Why were so many men here in the road? Why weren't they fighting the fire? Why were they milling around like men do when they have to go to court, or visit when somebody dies? An hour before, they had talked loud and fought the fire in a dead run.

They stood in little tight wads and whispered among themselves. Had the fire gone out? Smoke and fire covered every inch of the mountain, best I could tell.

I jerked my arm loose. "What about Dad? Where's he at?"

Some twenty men stood behind the truck--I didn't see Dad or Reek among them.

"Where's Dad?"

"Here," Dad said from the other side of the men. "I've got something to show you--you ain't gonna like it."

I saw the bodies lying on the ground; one was covered with Dad's old coat. The other one was covered with a ranger's green jacket.

"Is it Reek?" I go.

"Oh, no, he's lost his snuff can. He went across the branch to hunt for it."

Ceece's face was as white as a sheet when he saw the bodies. "Who, who, is they?"

"Gather around," the ranger said. "See if you know either of these men."

Dad reached down and pulled the coats from the charred faces. Although someone had wiped their faces, it was hard to tell what they had looked like.

Some more fire fighters walked by and studied the faces. Most shook their heads, and a few mumbled, "No."

After every man had looked, the ranger put the coats back over the dead men's faces. "That confirms it, they must be the ones that came up here in the spring and commenced making whiskey. Their still got cut down again last week."

"How did you find'em?" a firefighter asked Dad. "They must have set all the fires we thought were jumps."

"I figure the same," Dad said. "Later, we found that they'd stole a flame-thrower from one of the trucks and set fire at the mouth of that deep hollow. They couldn't out-run the fire, and when the flame-thrower blew up it led me to them."

The ranger-man got out a checkbook and laid it on the hood of his truck. "You men have been here from the onset. We have men from Tennessee and Georgia helping. They can finish mopping up. I'm going to pay you off right now and discharge you from this fire. The government can pay me back or go to hell."

Just like that, we were on Dad's truck headed toward home. Dad handed out the checks. Ceece didn't even look to see how much his was for. We hadn't gone more than five miles before raindrops as big as saucers hit us in the face.

More gems of the adventures of the now-familiar mountain family are here rendered in the same fireside-chat style that delighted readers of Bill Carver's stories in *Branch Water Tales*. The language spoken in the Southern Appalachian Mountains is lauded by some, lamented by others. There are those in our society, cloistered by various intellectual walls, who would obliterate the mountain dialect, and others who are attempting to "can" it for posterity. Carver, without pretense or presumption, presents the street language of the mountain byways as dialogue discernable by readers far afield. He provides the printed words that paint a vivid, dynamic, colorful mural of the doings of a people in a time that will soon be lost to living memory.

In these stories, Quill Vance, a mountain boy embroiled in transition, finds that truth is not always the operating mode of everyone doing business, yet he finds the senses of generosity, honesty, and fair play are not extinct. He discovers that the softness of girls is not limited to their feelings. He sees the sorrow and heartache that are caused by group and individual prejudice and bigotry. In struggles with powers of nature, where death seems imminent, he retains his sense of humor while he relies on heroic trust. When he sets out to earn a little money, he becomes entangled in a hilarious adventure that portends his social doom. His emotions are jerked and pummeled when he interacts with animals that animate the better of human traits, and with people who, some say, are worse than animals. While pursuing a favorite pastime, he becomes aware that personal and cultural values wear many cloaks.

--W.H. Massey, editor, Mountain Voice Publishers

The Author

Bill Carver is not a professor of anything, nor a possessor of expertise in any field. He writes what he has learned from a good, long life in these ancient mountains.

He writes solely for the joy of storytelling and the enjoyment of his readers. When you stop to study on it, that's not a bad calling.

Some More Branch Water Tales is Bill's latest book chronicling the adventures of a family in the Appalachian Mountains. *Branch Water Tales* begins the saga.